Walking in Darkness

Walking in Darkness

and other stories

C J Dacre

JAYSTONE PUBLICATIONS

Copyright © Jane Emerssen 2015
First published in 2015 by JayStone Publications, Bewdeill, Ashtree Avenue,
Keswick, Cumbria, CA12 5PF

www.jane-emerssen.co.uk

Distributed worldwide by Lightning Source

The right of Jane Emerssen to be identified as the author of the work has been
asserted herein in accordance with the Copyright, Designs and Patents Act 1988.

British Library Cataloguing in Publication Data
A catalogue record for this book is available from the British Library

ISBN 978-0-9574310-2-7

Typeset by Amolibros, Milverton, Somerset
www.amolibros.com
This book production has been managed by Amolibros
Printed and bound by Lightning Source

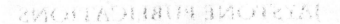

CONTENTS

ACKNOWLEDGEMENTS

'A Spanner in the Works' was first published in *Paperclips*, edited by Suzi Blair, published by New Fiction 1993.

'Such Stuff as Dreams are Made On' was originally published as 'Sixteen Tons' in *Northern Shorts*, edited by Suzi Blair, published by New Fiction 1993.

WALKING IN DARKNESS

"Hi Donald. Saw your skeeter come in. Sorry you couldn't make it sooner this time." The overly-affable hulk of the Photismian Station Security Chief, Lester Devine, swivelled round from the bank of surveillance monitors he'd been studying and shoved a spare chair across the office towards his visitor.

Ignoring the obvious gibe, MacKenzie dumped his travel sack and slouched bone-weary into the chair's functional, and far from luxurious, contour-support system. The mechanism groaned, he noticed, even under his own less bulky frame. Finally turning his mind to Devine's comment, he snapped open the pocket flap of his acclimatization suit and took out a hi-life. "Not much choice," he said, lighting up and inhaling deeply. "There's been a breakout over on Xanthus. Thought you'd have heard about it. All the connectors were ordered back to Arcadia II. I've been cooling my heels for the last ninety-six hours."

The Security Chief made a face feigning sympathy and pushed a disposal unit across to collect the ash threatening to collapse from the tip of MacKenzie's hi-life. "Those guys on Xanthus get all the action," he complained, casting a sideways glance in MacKenzie's direction. "What do I get? I get told to stay put while they call in a *Specialist*." His lips curled into a scowl. "And why? Cos I've got bloody boffins to keep an eye on – not slaggers." He evidently felt hard done by.

"You'd prefer a penal colony?" MacKenzie asked, squinting through a veil of smoke.

"Sure. Who the hell wants to baby-mind a load of crackpots? Give me the action where I can pull the trigger myself. I could put *you* lot out of a job in a fortnight," he added, jabbing a finger in MacKenzie's direction to emphasise his point.

MacKenzie refused to be drawn: he was used to Devine's ignorance – it was just par for the course. Being a Specialist was dangerous work. There was a 'high risk' rating on his insurance premium that cost him two months' salary every year – with no tax breaks either – something that got up his nose, but he couldn't do much about it. All part of the job. You couldn't get on Corporation listings as a Specialist without insurance.

Devine was talking again. "Well, down to business, eh? This is the latest one to go walkabout." He input a string of data into the console on the desk in front of him and handed over the official hologram image of a bearded, craggy-faced, dark-haired man that was spewed out a few seconds later. "Tannadyce," Devine said. "Just took off from the lab ten days ago."

"No warning?"

"Zilch – just like the rest of 'em." Devine brought up

the security footage for MacKenzie to watch. "That's him leaving the station on his last specimen expedition."

"Did he go out often?"

"Every couple of days or so. Nothing unusual – all the top lab rats do it – it's part of their job – looking for something new."

"So you wouldn't suspect anything was wrong?"

Devine shook his head. "Same routine – every time. Never varied."

"Except this time, he didn't come back."

Devine pulled a face. "Bloody typical," he said venomously. "They've all jiggered off when we're not expecting it."

MacKenzie drew hard on the hi-life, feeling more relaxed by the minute and less irritated by Devine's overfed condescension. He exhaled, the smoke spiralling upwards towards the ventilation unit which purred contentedly above him. "Haven't you found out yet why they do it?"

Devine laughed: an unpleasant, harsh sound with sadistic undertones. "Not my job," he said, leaning back heavily in his chair and clasping his thick ugly hands across his gross belly. "Leave that to the Devex head-shrinks. I just have to keep them 'safe' 'til they arrive."

MacKenzie couldn't help thinking Devine did an awful lot more than just keep them 'safe'. "And not ask any questions?" he probed, giving Devine the benefit of a raised eyebrow.

The laughter vanished from Devine's face as fast as it had appeared. He leaned forward across the desk again and jabbed a finger menacingly in MacKenzie's direction. "Like I said – it's not my job. Not *yours* either," he was at pains to point out, his eyes narrowing. "Don't you forget that. *You* just have to find him, give him a shot and bring him back alive. Nothing else."

MacKenzie smiled indulgently. "I think I might be able to manage that. I've brought them all back alive so far." And he had. All seven of them: Harker, Bujinski – and five others before them in the last three years. He wasn't even sure they'd needed the shot of lotus juice he'd pumped into them when he'd caught up with them. They'd have probably come quietly enough without it.

MacKenzie could never understand why Devex Corp was so hot on getting these crackpots back in the first place: none of them was any use afterwards. Talked gibberish. Not to mention what had happened to their eyes – a milky white film covering everything: irises; pupils – the lot. Rumour had it that the medics could find nothing clinically wrong. Hard to believe, if you'd seen it. Not that it mattered: they'd all suffered from premature ageing and died within a year. Pity about Bujinski though. She'd been top-shelf eye-candy by all accounts.

"Any other clues this time?" MacKenzie asked, tearing his attention away from the memories of Bujinski's soft, pliant body to the craggy features of the image in his hand, its intense, hawk-like eyes glaring back at him.

The big man shrugged, half-laughed and jerked a fat thumb towards the filtered windows. Beyond, a jungle of lush green vegetation constantly threatened the station perimeter fence. "If there are any, MacKenzie, they're out there."

"I mean...any clues from the top secret research Tannadyce was working on?"

Devine dropped his affability like a lump of lead. "How many times do I have to say this, MacKenzie? – there's no bloody top secret research going on up here!" He was very emphatic on this point. "Routine stuff – that's all – nothing else. All these goddam boffins do is work out how to generate enough energy to keep the UDC's necklace satellites in their orbit round Aramanthus." He stood up, towering over MacKenzie, his eyes bulging. He jerked his thumb again, this time at the monitors behind him. "Look at that lot," he said, glowering at the screens. "Four-thousand-five-hundred megametres of fenced-off plantation, churning out energy like there's no tomorrow. Top secret research programme? Like hell! Goddam gardeners – that's all I'm bloody minding!" He spat accurately into the disposal unit next to MacKenzie's elbow. The spittle fizzed and vanished in a wisp of steam.

MacKenzie eyed the accuracy of the hit with mild distaste. He wasn't sure the Alpha Grade Biotechs based on Photismos would agree with Devine's interpretation of their job descriptions. Giving Tannadyce's likeness a last glance, he stuffed the hologram into his travel sack along with the rest of his tack and got up. "Okay, I'll get started. Usual terms?" He looked the big man straight in the eye.

"Usual terms. Twenty-thousand now. Twenty-thousand when you bring him in."

MacKenzie input his access code on the terminal and brought up the deposit format on his account file. He punched in the first twenty-thousand and Devine verified. MacKenzie kept this eyes fixed firmly on the screen. "Was Tannadyce just another goddam gardener?" he asked casually, watching the message come up indicating that his account had been credited. The image in the hologram had been striking: there was something about the way the eyes looked right through you.

Devine shrugged, adopting an air of indifference. "How would I know? I'm just the bloody gate-keeper." He shrugged again. "He wasn't one for talking anyway. If I checked him out in the lab he'd be staring at the wall most of the time."

MacKenzie cleared the screen and flicked the last of his hi-life into the disposal unit. "Half-crazy already then?" he suggested casually.

"Yeah – probably."

MacKenzie noted Devine's smile restricted itself to his mouth.

★ ★ ★

In the sanitized deserted corridor outside Devine's office, MacKenzie smiled grimly at the surveillance camera and gave Devine a cheery wave to mask his innate dislike of the man. An irrational dislike, he told himself. After all, they both took the Corporation's money for doing a dirty job.

The reception zone, windowless and ablaze with harsh

white light from an obscured source, was silent save for the distant throb of the power plant. Surveillance equipment covered its every corner. Paranoia, thought MacKenzie.

Huge, brightly lit signs in garish red on either side of the grey, sealed doors laid down the rules to be followed if you wanted to get out of the place.

NO DEPARTURE ALLOWED WITHOUT
ACCLIMATIZER HELMET
IN PLACE
IN DARK-ROOM LOWER FILTER VISOR
NO EGRESS ALLOWED UNTIL VISOR IN PLACE
FOLLOW THESE INSTRUCTIONS!
EXTERNAL DANGER!

Only half-a-dozen or so acclimatizer helmets occupied the individually labelled lockers across one wall. He collected his helmet from the visitors' locker and lowered it into place. The air-conditioning whispered softly around him.

A surveillance camera above the door scanning personnel at point of departure gave him the once-over, noted his identity, and the huge grey panels slid open.

He stepped through into the dark-room, lit by a solitary red glow buried in the ceiling. The doors slid shut silently behind him and the red light went out. The darkness was oppressive.

Christ! It's as bad as being in space maintenance, MacKenzie reflected as he waited for the external door to open.

The infrared image sensor surveyed him critically. "You are about to exit the facility. Please lower your filter visor now," a female voice crooned through the ear phones. "The external door will not open until your visor is securely in place."

MacKenzie slammed the thing down, irritated by the reminder. Devine had unsettled him more than usual.

The external door slid back with a faint hum and MacKenzie stepped out into a brilliant, sunny day filled with the sounds that belonged uniquely to Photismos, sounds that were almost familiar to him now: the squawks, grunts, whistles, pings and a thousand other smaller noises as yet unidentified.

In the clearing immediately beyond the main gate, a platoon of robotic trimmers chattered mechanically to one another as they ceaselessly patrolled the perimeter fence. MacKenzie watched their dedicated progress. Programmed to keep the encroaching vegetation at bay, they followed their precise circuitous routes in pairs until they malfunctioned, to be replaced immediately by a constant supply of reserve machines.

Beyond the clearing and the plantation, the jungle rose up hundreds of metres into the sky. In its depths, the flora and fauna of Photismos continued to live in a state of perfect harmony, regarding the station buildings, the skeeter pad and the vast area of the energy plantation as a temporary hiccough in the planet's ecological system, waiting to be engulfed by the natural order of things at some time in the future.

Photismos. Discovered little more than a generation before by a five-man exploration cruiser out from Aramanthus, it was still shrouded in mystery. There were garbled rumours about what had actually happened to the crew, but the official records showed that four of the five had gone mad and died in less than a year later. They'd all suffered from blindness and premature ageing. It was something to do with the light, everyone said. If you didn't filter it, you went blind, crazy or both.

The fifth member – a man called Johannson, a Super-alpha Biotechnician with an IQ that defied quantification – had returned apparently unharmed. The myth grew up that he was already so weird in the head, his trip to Photismos hardly made any difference. But later, in conditions of unprecedented security, he'd developed an effective visor in his own workshop. In a moment of complete lunacy – or so it was said – he'd voluntarily offered the development rights to Devex. It was more likely he'd been coerced into handing them over under duress. After that, no one was very certain what had happened to him. The most popular version was that like the rest he eventually went blind and died a few years later in a Devex asylum, totally out of him mind. MacKenzie had heard something else entirely: Johannson had retired to a closed order up on Athena Minor, where he'd proceeded to dictate huge volumes of incomprehensible tracts, which Devex Corp could make no sense of whatever, despite numerous attempts to decode them. So they'd kept them locked away in their archives tagged as 'Protected Data'.

Whatever the truth, Devex had developed the visor at its top security research and development centre back on Earth, and then promptly bought up all the exploration franchises for Photismos from the Universal Development Commission. As a result, the UDC was now 100 per cent dependent on Devex Corp for all its energy requirements. There was no other way it could keep the satellite necklace in place as part of its major development project on Aramanthus – and it was having to pay through the nose for the privilege.

Devex had struck it rich. But why they should get the shakes so badly over missing biotechnicians – whatever their grade – MacKenzie had never been able to fathom out to his satisfaction.

Looking around him, it was hard to imagine what was so deadly about the light that bathed the Photismian landscape. The scene was one of tropical splendour, a riot of dense bright green foliage, of all shapes and sizes, rocketing skywards like the Amazonian Basin in a good season. Entwined lovingly around fleshy green trunks and branches were robust creepers smothered in flowers of every colour of the spectrum, from intense purples and blues to brilliant reds and yellows. And as they intertwined, they made soft, gasping exhalations, like lovers eternally reaching a climax.

Above the lush jungle, the sky was a brilliant cobalt blue with white fluffy clouds; and the single sun, slightly larger than the Earth's, glowed warmth and vitality onto its small, solitary planet, like an indulgent parent.

But if MacKenzie had ever been tempted to lift his visor

to get a better look at the confusion of colour around him, he'd only to remember the strange whiteness in the eyes of those he'd brought back. What in heaven's name had induced them to remove their visors to gaze out at this cornucopian landscape and accept the consequences? What terrible urge had made them opt for blindness, premature ageing, insanity, and certain death?

He shrugged, and turned his thoughts to more practical matters – which way to go?

There was no pattern to follow. None of the crazies had gone walkabout in the same direction. They'd just blundered out into the jungle to be picked up at random a few days later barely three or four megametres away from the station. The only single constant had been their universal decision to throw away not just their helmets and acclimatization suits, but every scrap of clothing as well. Then they'd sat down to stare at the world about them until they could stare no more. Remembering those blank, lifeless eyes made the hair on the back of MacKenzie's neck stand on end.

He surveyed the immediate area. There wasn't the slightest trace of Tannadyce's passing, which didn't surprise him.

Ten days was a long time in the life of the Photismian jungle. Too long. Nine-and-a-half days too long. Foliage snapped and trodden down in Tannadyce's flight would have begun to decay within minutes, producing that strong heady scent powerful enough to attract all the grazing gyraxes for megametres around. Snuffling and grunting, they'd have cleared up the debris in a twinkling, following in Tannadyce's wake like enthusiastic garbage collectors. Within twenty-four hours or so, renewed foliage and flowering exotica would have sprung up, blending in perfect harmony with the profusion already growing on every side.

Tannadyce had simply vanished without a trace.

So, it was back to instinct, thought MacKenzie. Plain, ordinary bloody instinct – and persistence. But that's what made him a Specialist.

He took out Tannadyce's image from his sack and studied it more closely. Those eyes. Come and get me, they taunted. MacKenzie felt his stomach tighten slightly under the intensity of that unflinching gaze.

Damn him, he thought, reading the mind behind the eyes. He's made for the hills.

The certainty of his hunch was as strong as it he had received confirmation in writing. He stuffed Tannadyce back in his sack and took out his hunting gear. He clamped the body-function sensors onto his belt and fixed the geofacsimile and compass next to them, then unhooking the laser trimmer from its sheath, he checked out its operational settings. Perfect. Lastly, he took stock of his ration levels and loaded the juice gun, placing it in the holster flap on his hip pocket.

Satisfied, he flicked on the trimmer switch and headed out across the clearing into the wall of jungle, the trimmer scything its way through the lush undergrowth barring his way. The vegetation sighed sadly as it fell.

A herd of fawn-like, graceful three-horned optillas, busily browsing on a decaying stump, turned to watch his passing with their huge sorrowful white eyes. If they had not moved, MacKenzie would never have noticed their presence.

Like all the planet's fauna, optillas changed colour at will. Not for reasons of camouflage. Optillas had no use for camouflage. None of the Photismian fauna had: there were no predators to guard against. They simply chose to harmonize with their surroundings – or anyway, that was the theory. Browsing through the jungle, coughing softly as they went, they echoed the dappled brilliance of adjacent foliage from the base of their cloven hooves to the tips of their multi-ridged horns. At first glance, it was hard to distinguish them from their surroundings, except for their strange, white ovoid eyes that stared out blankly at the garish, multi-coloured world around them.

MacKenzie scythed on. Already he could hear the first grunts and snuffles of the grotesquely-snouted gyraxes behind him as they scented the decaying stems felled by the trimmer. He pressed ahead, not looking back, harvesting as he went.

★ ★ ★

Five days out, the ground showed signs of rising as he reached the foothills. Although the going was easier as he gained altitude with increasing breaks in the canopy, the sensors on the tracking indicator had shown a human zero on every test-sounding he'd made. Most of the blips and zings thrown onto the screen emanated from a particular species of tree creeper which had evolved a valve in its basal stem that functioned in much the same way as the human heart. Other traces came from a lesser species, where small electrical impulses registered – almost like thoughts – as they considered whether to twine to the right, or twine to the left. The host involved would oblige by prompting, moving a branch slightly in one direction or another to assist a decision. This branch-flexing also had a habit of showing up on the sensors, adding to the confusion of patterns splattered across the screen.

MacKenzie stopped every few megametres, sifting and analysing, hoping that at least one of the myriad combinations he was looking at was the faintest echo of a human being.

But there was nothing.

By the seventh day, he'd been out in the Photismian jungle for longer than ever before. The rhythm of the laser trimmer and steady crunch, crunch of his boots on fleshy stalks, had begun to lull his brain, and the constant cloying smell from dying vegetation was beginning to seep through the acclimatizer seams, filling his nostrils with its sickly odour. He could even taste it.

The exertion of climbing was adding to his discomfort and his head had become strangely light, as if he'd smoked too many hi-lifes at one go. He trudged on, noticing his movements had developed an automatic, almost dream-like quality, taking him steadily onwards and upwards towards the main thrust of the hills which now towered above him through breaks in the canopy. His concentration was somewhere else entirely.

With considerable effort, he forced himself to stop

dead in his tracks, labouring hard to clear his head. He gazed down abstractedly at the body-function sensors for the umpteenth time, conscious of readings that needed interpreting and a mind too fogged to differentiate between plant and animal, and – what was more disconcerting – not giving a damn. Instead, he found himself listening with a hypnotic fascination to the din of the jungle flora and fauna around him.

He smiled to himself for no particular reason. Tannadyce had become a meaningless goal. He could no longer remember why he was looking for him. He patted his travel sack for clues and found nothing helpful. He checked the hip holster and found the presence of the juice gun vaguely comforting, although the reason for carrying it remained stubbornly elusive.

A leucoptid dicephalo, minding its own herbivorous business munched noisily twenty metres or so above him, snorted, and idly moved forward to its next delectable leafy meal. It advanced, oblivious of his minuscule presence, its smooth oily skin rippling with emerald green and vermilion in homage to a nearby exotic creeper.

MacKenzie looked up, watching the six huge trunk-like legs pushing forward through the undergrowth towards him, stems popping and keeling over under the inexorable advance. He knew he should do something – make some attempt to avoid the seemingly inevitability of being crushed to death. But his limbs felt heavy and unwieldy. He could barely move them.

With a supreme effort, he slewed himself sideways.

His foot snagged in the roots of a giant weed, and he experienced the strange sensation of falling in ultra-slow motion. As he fell, he watched, fascinated, as the laser trimmer flew out of his grasp, arcing gracefully through the air to vanish into the depths of a nearby dark green pool with a barely audible 'plop'. The ripples fanned outwards in a series of perfect concentric circles.

Above him, one dicephalo head whistled softly to the other and the beast changed direction, its attention diverted by a more mouth-watering morsel elsewhere.

MacKenzie lay sprawled flat out for what might have been a minute or a lifetime – it mattered little. He listened, his breath rasping harshly in his ears, coming in short, staccato bursts.

Clumsily, he struggled to his feet, fumbling for the juice gun and clutching it in a vain attempt to steady his jangled nerves. The stench of decaying vegetation had become stronger than ever. It seemed to have become part of him, seeping in and out through the very pores of his skin – like too much alcohol or garlic. Drunkenly, he stumbled on, flailing his arms in front of him to clear a way. The soft fleshy stems snapped and popped as he careered forward.

Twice he fell, the second time face down into a shallow, stagnant pool where his grip on the juice gun slackened and it fell away into the rotting sediment unnoticed.

He pulled himself out onto the bank, wiping away the haze of decaying vegetation soup smeared across his visor. He was winded and his heart was pumping blood across his temples in a primitive incessant drumbeat that made his head feel like an over-ripe melon ready to burst. Perspiration had sprung out on his forehead and stayed there, despite the cooling system in his suit.

Clumsily, he pawed at the visor, unable to understand why his vision was still so badly clouded. Then realisation dawned – condensation was building up inside his helmet. His cooling system had failed. Before long, it would be impossible for him to see anything clearly enough to go on.

Pure panic screwed up his stomach into a tight little knot. He could hear himself whimpering like a sick dog. Wildly, he clawed at the helmet, yanking the clasps free and dragging at the safety catches. There was a snapping sound and the helmet sprang off its mountings and fell away somewhere onto the ground.

The light burst in on him.

At first, his eyes refused to transmit what he was seeing. Nothing made sense. And then everything shot into brilliant, pin-sharp focus, and he heard his breath, already uneven and disjointed, begin to quicken and expand until it streamed out of him in an ear-piercing crescendo of sound that sent unseen things scuttling away in every direction. It echoed away and around the encroaching hills, bouncing backwards and forwards; whirling around his head like a maddened bird, until he dropped to his knees sobbing uncontrollably.

The helmet! For God's sake where was it?

Gathering what was left of his wits, he smothered his face with one hand and scrabbled around in the thick mushy softness of the decaying mess with the other. His fingers foraged, groping frantically in their desperate search. But the helmet and its visor refused to be found.

He fumbled uselessly for what seemed like a small eternity, until defeated and crushed, he fell face down into the rotting stench about him and retched. Bile spewed out of his slack mouth and sank quietly into the fetid waters of the shallow pool beside him.

He lay, devoid of thought: exhausted.

Somewhere close above his head, a strong but reassuring male voice spoke to him. "There's nothing to fear," it said simply.

MacKenzie lifted his head slowly, screwing up his eyes. Behind closely shuttered lids, he could just make out the figure of a naked man.

"Tannadyce?" he whispered hoarsely.

"If you like." The man bent forward and helped him to his feet, gripping his arm with encouraging firmness.

MacKenzie stood on legs unwilling to support his weight, conscious of his teeth chattering in his head. "Will – will I go blind? Tell me I won't go blind!"

Tannadyce didn't answer immediately. "They'll think you have," he said at last, keeping a firm hold on MacKenzie's trembling limbs.

MacKenzie could hear himself sobbing while Tannadyce's reassuring voice talked over and through the din in his head.

"It's not easy to explain," Tannadyce was saying. "Soon you'll see more – understand better." He squeezed MacKenzie's arm. "Trust me. Open your eyes. Once you've seen everything, you'll begin to understand. Believe me. Open your eyes."

Seduced by Tannadyce's calm insistence, and dimly aware he hadn't the mental or physical strength to refuse, MacKenzie slowly opened his eyes, blinking like an idiot as his brain tried to unravel the myriad contradictions that assailed him.

He was staring out at a light-inverted world.

Scarlet and luminous red foliage soared upwards all around him like the flames of a vast forest fire, the flowers on the creeper stems the deepest greens and browns. Bewildered, he looked upwards. Above him, the sky was a rich golden-yellow, reflecting itself in the dark-ochre pool at his feet; and emerging from behind an iron-grey fluffy cloud, a midnight-blue sun blazed down, casting white shadows on the ground.

Tannadyce's grip on his arm tightened a little to steady him. MacKenzie turned to face him – unprepared for what he saw.

Tannadyce no longer looked remotely like a human being. He'd been transformed into something that belonged to macabre folklore tales of Bogey-men and the Undead. His skin was greenish-blue like that of a corpse too long in water; his wild, bedraggled hair and unkempt beard were a strange greyish white.

"My God!" MacKenzie heard himself say as he fixed his gaze on Tannadyce's eyes. The sockets stared back at him with an unblinking inky blackness that made the man's face look like a skull: it was a ghastly, terrifying image. "Am I going mad?"

"No, you're not," Tannadyce assured him. "*This* is reality." There was a note of wonderment in his voice as he turned, encompassing everything around them with an expansive sweep of his arm. "Soon I shall understand *everything*." He paused and turned his unholy black sockets back on MacKenzie again. "And now you've seen the light," he added quietly, "so will you."

"No!" MacKenzie protested, "No! Let me go!" But the harder he tried to escape Tannadyce's vice-like grip, the stronger the hypnotic hold of his hideous eyes became. They riveted him; bored into him; and transfixed him where he stood. He could feel himself slowly melting away. Tannadyce seemed to be pouring into his brain, scouring every nook and cranny inside his head. He was being wiped clean. Remade. Soon there would be nothing left of his former self except his Being. "Please," MacKenzie begged, "I don't want to go mad!"

Tannadyce smiled. "What is madness – " he said, "but the gift of the gods?"

MacKenzie could hear himself sobbing like a child, weak and defenceless against the apparent inevitability of fate.

"There's nothing to fear," Tannadyce insisted, his voice, if he spoke at all – and MacKenzie was no longer sure that he had – seemed to come from very far away. "Accept what you've been given," it said, "and be glad."

For a moment, MacKenzie thought he was dying, his head spinning, his vision blurring into blackness, and the sound of thunder clamouring in his ears. Then silence – and a very definite moment of infinite calm. A flood of consciousness began swimming into his brain like a torrent released from a broken dam: swirling; churning; filling him up. There was no more panic. No sense of fear. He was ready. He was waiting. He'd been an empty vessel needing to be filled. "What do I tell them?" he heard himself ask.

"Say you couldn't find me, that's all."

"They won't believe me."

"Does it matter?" Tannadyce stooped and retrieved the battered helmet from behind a flame-coloured bush and wiped the visor free of filth with an oversized scarlet leaf. "Here. Take it."

"Is there much point?"

"You'll need time to readjust – to start again."

Like an obedient child, MacKenzie let Tannadyce fix the helmet back onto its mountings and lower the visor. Through the filter, Tannadyce and the crazy world he'd chosen to inhabit slipped back into their artificial reality. Or almost. Tannadyce's eyes, pure white – every bit of them – eyeballs, irises, pupils – as white as snow – fixed him with the seemingly blind unflinching gaze of an optilla. Try as he might, MacKenzie couldn't mask the horror he felt at the sight of them – or the knowledge that this strange and altered state would soon be his fate too. "Why did you come out?" he asked. It suddenly seemed important to know the answer.

Tannadyce looked mildly surprised by the question. "Curiosity," he said. "Scientists are curious creatures. What is it about Photismian light that generates so much energy?

The answer had to be out here – and perhaps it would be something beyond our understanding."

"And that was the only reason? – curiosity?"

"Yes – at first."

"But you all knew what would happen if you did."

"Physically and mentally – yes. Intellectually – no." Tannadyce turned to cast his seemingly sightless eyes once more over the landscape around them. "We came out searching for the truth and discovered much more. Perhaps we all had the same desire to be part of this strangely beautiful interdependence. To live a life of exquisite harmony with nature – however short or long that life might be. Perhaps Photismos chooses to call those it needs to cherish it."

"I wasn't called," MacKenzie pointed out.

Tannadyce turned back to look at him once more. "Weren't you?" he asked with a smile. "Perhaps you were – you just didn't recognise it."

MacKenzie vaguely remembered studying the image of Tannadyce in Devine's office and fleetingly sensing something indefinable. "Your hologram?" he asked.

Tannadyce nodded.

"But why? I don't understand."

"I've been blessed with ultimate knowledge. But only when I comprehend everything fully, will I be able to keep Photismos safe from any further human exploitation. Until then no one must find me. I knew you were the only one who could." He smiled apologetically. "So I had to call you – and forge this unbreakable bond between us."

"What am I supposed to do?"

"Just go back – and wait. Set your mind free. Open up. Accept. Then you'll see everything – understand everything – as I do. Go now, and be happy."

Obediently, MacKenzie turned to leave, casting one last look behind him at the wild figure standing alone amidst the jungle flora – a new Adam in Eden. "Will we meet again?" he asked.

"When you're ready."

MacKenzie turned and stumbled away, pushing into the depths of the greenery he knew to be vermilion and orange; past sky-blue pools of dazzling yellow; through dappled sunlight of midnight hues and into obsidian shadows of the purest white.

* * *

Two weeks later, led by instinct alone, he made it back to the perimeter fence, bedraggled and in a state of semi-delirium. Devine suspected him of dosing himself with lotus juice rather than admit defeat.

Devex Security ordered controlled isolation for six months with appropriate psychiatric treatment, and authorised the docking of ten-thousand from MacKenzie's account pending medical diagnosis. But the medics could get no sense out of him: his knowledge was locked away inside garbled brain patterns. After they had tried everything in the book – and more besides – they confined him to the isolation unit in the Secure Zone on the far side of the station out of harm's way: a frightening white-eyed senile figure, who had aged thirty years in one.

He spent his last days sitting in a favourite chair smiling benignly at the scene beyond the filtered windows and ignoring the paramedics who tended his ailing frame. He was beyond them all.

"Of course, he can't see anything," they said to casual visitors. "Just like the others."

MacKenzie smiled to his inner self. He could see just as well as before. In fact much better. He could understand better too. Now he had the knowledge to understand why Devex had been so hot to retrieve its personnel. Johannson's complex tracts had given them a clue there was more to be had from Photismos besides it phenomenal plant-based energy. And Devex was determined to find out what it was. Hence the need for a Specialist, the over-enthusiastic debriefings and psychiatric probes.

But MacKenzie had learned the art of shutting off his knowledge.

Had Harker reached this blessed state? Had Bujinski? Had they seen everything – as he now did? – allowing the total dedication of their mental faculties to take precedence over their physical maintenance and renewal? Had they too kept Photismos safe from Devex out of choice? – feigning insanity to match their premature ageing? Or had their new-found knowledge really blown their minds? Would that be his fate too? Surely only an intellect with the capacity of a Johannson or Tannadyce could withstand the onslaught of so much knowledge and survive? Johannson had been the signpost. Tannadyce had followed his path: his intellect would expand until he become Absolute Knowledge itself. The Ultimate Existence.

MacKenzie pondered on the beauty of human life. He gazed with an abstract fascination at the ageing skin on the backs of his hands, down to the basal germinating layers; and further, down to the veins beneath that formed the radial arteries and superficial palmer arches, and the long strands of the ulnar and median nerve cells; and still further, through the interweaving layers of abductor minimi digiti and abductor pollicis brevis muscles to the bones themselves, the metacarpals and phalanges, the trapezia and carpi; and on, even into the medullary vessels, to watch the red and white corpuscles at play. Soon – perhaps tomorrow – he would begin to see their atomic structure and the beginnings of life itself.

He lifted his head, conscious of its increasing weight, and stared out of the windows. Filtered though they were, he could see it all; just as the dicephalos, gyraxes and optillas saw it. As Tannadyce saw it. As perhaps Harker and Bujinski had seen it. Perfect. A blending. The mingling and interdependence of life forms. Flora and fauna. One and the same. A whole indivisible symbiosis. An immaculate mutualism. Paradise.

In the darkness that was light, MacKenzie listened to the creation of the universe within his brain with a quiet ecstasy. He let the knowledge flow freely, exulting in its ability to amaze and delight; and somewhere afar off, he heard his name being called very softly.

"Can I come now?" he asked silently.

"Soon," came the gentle reassuring reply.

And he accepted the instruction with the same calm unquestioning resignation that would in time lead him out through the perimeter fence and beyond, to join the others in an everlasting, joyful transfiguration.

A SPANNER IN THE WORKS

"What's the damage?" Stevens' neutral voice asked him over the headset.

Harris braced himself against the bulkhead and executed a half-twist, craning his neck, his forehead pressed hard against the observation panel to give him maximum visibility. Earthshine glinted along the length of the nose cone and forward sections, smooth at first, then stopping abruptly, burying itself in deep shadow before re-emerging, sleek and brilliant – as though nothing had happened.

"A fair-sized dent just behind the flight-deck for starters," Harris reported, swivelling awkwardly in the restricted space to check the solar-panel gantry behind the cargo hold. It was a mess: one half twisted back on itself almost 30° out of alignment. "Looks like the solar fins took the ricochet," he added, marvelling at his ability for understatement.

"Anything else?"

"Isn't that enough?" He scanned the rest of the visible area: nothing. With difficulty he eased himself down into the payload bay, its racking stacked high with crated scientific equipment that should have been winging its way to Skylab

V – and wasn't. He activated the door leading onto the flight-deck.

Stevens – Pilot Grade One and about as friendly as an iceberg – was standing with her back to him as he entered, her head with its close-cropped auburn hair bent forward over the control console. She turned as she heard him approach. Her face was impassive.

"I thought this was a clear-way," Harris commented drily.

Stevens turned back to the monitor. "It is – according to the data." She pointed to a string of survey reports on the screen. "Cleaned up seven years ago. No debris. No space junk. No projected meteorite storms in the next six days. Nothing."

Harris jerked a thumb over his shoulder and snorted. "That's one hell of a lot of nothing that just hit us back there!"

She raised an eyebrow.

He swore under his breath. "So why didn't it show up on the scanners?"

She shrugged, as though the matter was of no consequence to her. "Perhaps its profile was too small – maybe too smooth." She shrugged again.

"So where does that leave us?" he demanded.

Stevens drew in long breath and let it go very slowly. "On course for burn-up," she said simply.

"No power?"

"Not enough to activate the auxiliary drive." She turned back to the console. "Whatever hit us left us with just enough to keep our vital systems ticking over until we're rescued – or fried to a crisp."

"How long before re-entry?"

Stevens casually read from an adjacent screen, its bright display of fluorescent green numbers reducing remorselessly. "If the rescue shuttle doesn't reach us – and I'm told there's a fifty-fifty chance it won't – six hours thirty-seven minutes – and two seconds."

Harris felt sweat break out on his forehead. "And we just sit here – and do nothing?"

"What do you suggest?"

"I could have a crack at re-orientating the fins," he volunteered.

"No," she said decisively, "that would be contrary to Cruiser Fleet Regulations. You know that. Only classified spaceworkers can go external. Regulation 28."

"I'm a qualified Technical Officer, for god's sake. I'd rather be out there doing something than sitting in here watching those bloody seconds tick by!" He was shouting now and he didn't care.

"You're not a classified spaceworker," she insisted, her rigid interpretation of the rules stalling him as it had on other occasions. "I'd have to go out there with you."

"Like hell you would!" he said, forgetting protocol. "If I'm out there, I want to know someone's still manning the bridge. I'll just have to learn to be a big boy on my own."

"Like Champion?"

"Champion didn't follow the safety regs."

"Will *you*?"

They glared at one another across the confined space of the flight-deck.

"Are you going to get me sanction to go EVA or not?" he demanded.

She eyed him coldly for a moment, then nodded. "Get suited up and log-out Champion's toolkit. I'll contact Control."

Saluting, Harris ducked back into the payload bay. He looked up briefly. Through the observation panel the buckled gantry towered above him, a menacingly ugly silhouette. He turned from it quickly, digging out from the storage locker Champion's box of tricks.

Champion's cherished toolkit was all they'd managed to salvage from the accident, hauling it back on its security line. Everything had happened so fast: a routine maintenance check that went horribly wrong, and Champion had spun off into space, his lifeline severed by the air-lock door.

Harris bent down, snapping open the catches of the casing to check off the contents against the inventory engraved on the lid. It was a chore he should have completed as soon as the box had been recovered. *Cruiser Fleet Regulation 148. Paragraph 4. Incidents: Items of maintenance equipment MUST be accounted for by the recovering officer.* He hadn't. Instead, for almost a whole orbit he'd had a stand-up row with Stevens over the merits of recovering Champion's body – and like so many other times he'd failed to move her – a failure that still rankled. He'd liked Champion.

He eased back the toolkit lid and stopped, staring stupidly into the contents. His eyes glazed. Seconds seemed to expand themselves into hours, stretching out with a dreadful slowness as his brain sifted through a thousand-and-one disjointed, perplexing memories. And then he understood.

He jolted back into reality, his vision clearing, bringing with it the awful truth. Before him lay a glaringly empty compartment, testimony to his negligence: the multi-purpose wrench was missing.

Slowly, inexorably, Harris felt his stomach starting to tie itself up into a tight little knot. He looked up at the accusing, distorted outline of the solar fins above him, and grimaced.

IT WON'T HURT A BIT

"What did we try last time?"

"Milo-3658."

"And that was definitely not right?"

"Definitely."

The medic looked puzzled, squinting at the densely-packed list of possibilities on the screen. His lips moved silently as he mentally ticked off the items they'd tried before. "I can't understand it," he said, shaking his head at the·improbable possibility someone had blundered. "We were 99.9 per cent certain we'd hit on the right one this time."

Howard stared up at the ceiling from his recumbent position on the examination couch and took particular interest in the light fitting directly over his head. Patience was a virtue he'd never possessed. That's why he was absolutely certain that Milo-3658 was the wrong memory bank. He was being very patient. "Look," he said after the silence had gone on for at least four more minutes, "I don't want to make a big thing of this, but hey, this is the twenty-seventh time you've said that."

The medic looked distinctly pained at having to be reminded about this. "We're doing our best," he countered, his eyes darting back to the screen apparently seeking reassurance from the welter of information scrolling up at considerable speed.

"Okay, I understand that, but how many more possibilities are there?"

"Hard to say."

"A rough estimate?"

The medic just shrugged, avoiding eye-contact.

"You mean you haven't the foggiest?"

"No – not exactly."

"So what's the story so far?"

"Well – we've run through the obvious – numeric inversions, input errors – upwards and downwards, accidental alphanumeric insertions –"

"And I'm still missing?" Howard couldn't help sounding just a little incredulous.

The medic cleared his throat. "A lot of data got scrambled in the System melt-down last year," he explained, with a tight-lipped smile.

Howard considered this for a moment and sighed. "You mean you've really no idea who I am?"

"Oh, it's not as bad as that," the medic was keen to reassure him. "We're pretty certain from other factors that you're a Milo."

Howard sighed again, sat up and swung his legs over the side of the couch. "You mean you're 99.9 per cent certain?"

The medic frowned at him. "You shouldn't sit up while you're still linked into the System," he warned. "It could trigger a malfunction."

"Well that could be an improvement on the current situation, don't you think?"

"This isn't a matter for levity, Mr Milo."

Howard casually disconnected the electrodes from the plug-in points on his temples and waggled his toes, watching them with undue fascination. "You know something?" he said after a moment's reflection, " – I couldn't agree more. But let's face it, you're no nearer rebooting my history than you were six months ago when I came in here."

"Your tag was damaged – that wasn't our fault."

"Well it definitely wasn't mine. I was out cold. If the Facility can't manage a crisis, that's something they need to look into. I could've been killed."

The medic didn't respond to this.

"Look, is there any chance I could pop out for a while and get something to eat?"

The idea was greeted with horror.

"Okay – only joking. But how much longer is this session going to take? I mean, would there be any harm in my pottering around here for a couple of days as Milo-3658 and coming back when you've talked things over with a supervisor?"

"I – I don't think that's a good idea."

"Can you come up with a better one?"

The medic winced.

"You see, I look at it this way," Howard said, sensing he might just have tapped into something that had briefly flitted through the medic's thought processes as well. "All this wrong history stuff is really getting to me. I've got a head full of almost-memories –"

"Echoes," the medic corrected him.

"Well, okay – echoes. I'm getting *really* confused. I don't want to keep adding to them."

The medic nodded. "Understandable," he said, looking seriously concerned.

"So I'd be really grateful if you'd just give me a break and take some time to sort things out. I mean – have you any idea how complicated life can be when you've got so much stuff over-written in your head? It can get into a real mess. Like spaghetti. Okay, I'll admit I didn't mind catching up on all the theoretical possibilities of astrophysics from Milo-8365 because I was rubbish at it in college, but his sex-life was Alpha Grade zilch. And then there was that weirdo Milo-5368 – what the hell was he up to? Not to mention Milo-356B. I mean – with all this hair on my chest – do I really look like a girl?"

The medic was visibly peeved at him raising this again. "We've already apologised for that error, Mr Milo," he said curtly. "It was a regrettable mismatch."

"Well, I'm glad to hear you say that, because frankly, you had me worried for a while." Howard's attention was deflected by the interesting way he could describe a circle by simply moving the ankle of his right foot in a particular way.

The medic was still pondering the possibility of deferring any further intervention without getting it in the neck from someone higher up the pecking order.

"What do you think then?" Howard said, feeling things couldn't be left just as they were. "I can get by with Milo-3658 for a couple more days. Okay, he's not me, but he's a nice enough guy – not very interesting, but hey, I can live with that."

"I don't know."

"Go on – give me a break."

The medic looked beaten. "You know you won't be able to leave the Medical Facility?"

Howard surveyed the half-dressed state he was in and shrugged. "Do I look as though I could go anywhere else?"

"As long as you understand."

"Fine by me. When do you want me back?"

"I'll call you when we've studied all the options."

"Could be a week or two then?"

The medic glared at him but said nothing.

★ ★ ★

The only useful piece of information Howard could honestly remember with any sense of clarity these days was the reassurance that – "It won't hurt a bit." It never did, so there was nothing different about this or any of the other mismatched personal history implant procedures.

There was the usual whirring in his ears that reached a high-pitched whine as the blood flow quickened, and trillions of memory impulses flooded through his cerebral cortex, triggering myriad synapse responses, reconfiguring, re-routing and rebooting his hippocampus. It could almost be described as exhilarating, like white-water rafting, or competing in the downhill slalom – something one of his Milo counterparts had done regularly apparently – but it played havoc with his energy reserves. Afterwards, he was always as weak as a kitten and usually out of things for a couple of days curled up on his bunk like a hibernating dormouse.

After that, they'd disconnect him from the System and he'd wake up to a whole new world.

At first the memories came thick and fast. They were vivid; intense; almost believable, except they weren't, because they weren't his. His life was suddenly populated by people, places and personal attributes he couldn't empathise with or recall, no matter how hard he tried.

Wiping out the mismatch before re-implantation worked a couple of times, but from then on, hazy recollections of his 'other' lives began to interleave themselves into each successive rebooting. Occasionally, he caught himself pondering the veracity of an exquisite equation without the faintest notion of what it represented. And then there was the serious matter of day-dreaming about the pleasure of sticking pins into various extremely sensitive parts of his anatomy, not to mention the sudden interest he'd developed in female fashion accessories and the sexual potential of every passing male. It was no laughing matter. He was seriously beginning to question whether he'd ever get rid of these false memories at all.

And as for who he really was...

"Hi," a bright young female said, sitting down next to him in the Bistro Bar with a maxi-meal. "You in the same boat?" she asked, indicating her own version of the garb he was wearing.

Taken aback by the unexpected interest in him by a

member of the opposite sex – and a pretty one at that – Howard wasn't entirely sure what she meant. He'd a fleeting memory of being rescued from a sailing dingy as a small child, except of course, it hadn't been him.

She was laughing at him, tugging at his sleeve. "They can't find me either," she said tucking into her meal with more enthusiasm than Howard could muster for his.

"Really? I thought I was the only one."

She shrugged this off. "How many times have they tried with you?"

"Twenty-seven."

Her lavender-blue eyes widened in horror. "You're joking!"

He shook his head. His heart felt leaden. Here was another lovely opportunity to make things happen. He'd had so many. Or rather, Milo-3658 once had, but they'd all gone wrong. He'd just have to accept the sad fact he wasn't interesting enough. Maybe it was something to do with being in sewerage decontamination management. Whatever.

"I've only had four," she was saying cheerily, apparently unfazed by this. "Been quite an experience," she added with a knowing look in his direction. "How about you?"

"Can't say I'm enjoying it."

She thought about this. "I'll probably feel the same," she said after a moment's reflection. "The excitement'll wear off after a bit, I suppose."

Howard concentrated hard on his plate of whatever-it-was, wishing he could summon up some sparkling conversation, knowing he'd not a cat in hell's chance of achieving anything remotely humorous, or witty.

"Do you get multi-recalls?" she was asking him, suddenly serious.

He nodded.

"I just wondered. I mean, do they keep coming?"

He nodded again.

She lost interest in her meal and pushed it aside, leaning closer. "I've just had my first," she confessed. "I thought maybe, well – you know, maybe it was a one off."

He shook his head.

"Is it that bad?"

"Not exactly *bad*. Just confusing." He didn't want to go into the finer detail of some of the less attractive aspects. No point in frightening the horses, as Rankin would have said.

Who the hell was Rankin?

She was nodding, understandingly, slipping back into a more mischievous mood. "I think they might let me stick with the latest version," she said brightly. "I don't mind. I rather like her. What do you think?"

Howard smiled at her optimistically, hoping this was what she wanted. "Well, you're very nice," he offered. "Does that help?"

She positively glowed. "Enormously. Oh, by the way," she added, offering him her hand to shake. "I'm Sandra Milo – or I think that's who I am at the moment."

Howard listened to the echo in his head. "You're not Milo-356B by any chance?"

Her face lit up with undisguised merriment. "Oh – don't tell me – you've not been me, have you?"

Howard nodded apologetically, as if somehow this had been his fault.

She leaned over and kissed him lightly on the cheek, filling his head with the most delightful perfume. "Oh you poor thing," she said, all desperate concern and sympathy. "How could they do that? That's horrible."

He shrugged it off, pretending to make light of it.

Her concern evaporated. She leaned closer, whispering so that no one else sitting at the bar could hear, "Haven't I got the most atrocious taste in underwear?"

Howard could feel himself turning bright red.

She laughed softly. "So you *do* remember that. My, my – what else do you remember?"

Howard tried very hard not to recall too much, which was difficult now that he had an identifiable human being to pin his recollections to. He'd no intention of divulging anything too dramatic. Milo-3658 would consider this downright ungentlemanly. "You're a Grade 3 Technician in Reconstruction," he said, keeping himself in check. "You've been in the Facility for five years. Promoted twice. You like dancing, the latest fashions – and white-water rafting. Er – no, that was someone else."

She was delighted. "Anything else?"

Howard decided she was definitely goading him. He shook his head, avoiding the possibility she might be sizing him up as a bed-mate. That would be too much to hope for.

She sighed and let the subject drop. "So who are you at the moment?"

"Milo-3658. I'm a boring thirty-four-year-old in sewerage decontamination management."

The last part of this information seemed to pass her by. "What happened?" she asked. "I mean, why did you need rebooting?"

"Something to do with the electromagnetic surge in the Distribution Centre. They've reconfigured everyone else apparently – except me. My tag got damaged, and the Indexing Unit's had a major melt-down, so all they've got to go on is I'm listed somewhere under Milo. They just can't find me. What about you?"

"Oh, it was that thing with the Integrated Research Unit last year – when it exploded. I'm the only one they were able to reconstruct properly. It's taken ages, but they've done a pretty good job, don't you think?"

He could only agree that they had.

"They say they've got ten Identities to work through. At least you know who you're supposed to be. I've absolutely no idea who I am. What's the betting I turn out to be Number Ten?" She laughed at this but Howard sensed she didn't find it particularly funny. "What's your other name?" she asked suddenly. "Do you know?"

"Howard."

"Pleased to meet you, Howard," she said, and without pausing asked enthusiastically, "Anything planned for the rest of the day?"

"Taking a break from being too many different people,"

he said, noticing his attention was shifting to the attractive way her cheeks formed dimples when she laughed.

"Well, I suppose I'm doing the same. I got a bit panicky when I had a recall moment – you know, one of those – what do they call them?"

"Echoes."

"Echoes," she repeated. "So they all went into a huddle and decided it might be better to give me the rest of the day off. One of them was very twitchy. I heard him say – 'that's the second one today' – and they all went very quiet."

"Maybe I got you off the hook," he suggested, feeling this might put him in a good light.

She beamed at him. "Hey – maybe you did."

Howard's mind slipped into a blank – a Milo-3658 blank associated with chatting up members of the opposite sex. He sat staring at the top of the bar wondering what the hell he could say next. She'd have absolutely no interest in the complexities of sewerage decontamination, and for that matter, he'd no idea what they were anyway, so that was a non-starter. Astrophysics wasn't going to do anything for her either, that much he remembered, and he'd no intention of suggesting she might like to stick pins into him. But he knew what *she* was thinking. Milo-365B was definitely sizing him up.

"I was just wondering," she began tentatively, linking her arm through his, "as we're both at a bit of a loose end at the moment...what do you say to spending the rest of the afternoon in my bunk?"

Somewhere through the fug of confused and jumbled

up memories littering his brain, Howard could remember someone not unlike Sandra slipping out of her jumpsuit and climbing into bed with him. She'd been fantastic.

"It wouldn't hurt, would it?" she was asking him.

"Not a bit," he said.

A VERY SHELTERED UPBRINGING

By the way, my name's Nigel Warburton. Thanks for explaining about the manure.

Granddad didn't believe in wasting things either. *Waste not want not*, he used to say. I was upset when he died – New Year's Eve. I couldn't think of anything useful to do with him. Thought about it for days. Then I remembered what he would've said. *If in doubt, look it up.* So I did.

In Volume 4 CON – EDU under **Dead, Disposal of the**, it said, 'Living with putrefying corpses is unhygienic.' But under the circumstances it was a bit difficult getting rid of him. I mean, I couldn't dig a hole or burn him, could I? And I hadn't got the right chemicals to turn him into compost. I thought eating him might be best but by then it was the seventh of January and he smelt a bit funny. I suppose the hydrolysis of his proteins into amino-acids had got going in a big way by then.

I got quite carried away with the suggested 'further reading', but the funerary rites in aboriginal communities didn't seem very practical either. So there was nothing for it but the disposal unit. He'd shrunk a lot anyway, so there was less of him to get rid of.

Fig 1 under **Skeleton** in Volume 12 ROS – SPA was useful. It was messy though – and the smell turned my stomach. I used the hacksaw, but I think I should have cut him into smaller pieces because the unit made a funny grunging noise when it was chomping up the femurs and didn't work very well after that. The floor took ages to get clean as well.

Pity I couldn't have eaten him.

I missed having him to talk to. I suppose that's why I came up.

We went down in December 1979 – just after Christmas. I was five. The Russians invaded Afghanistan and Granddad said the Americans wouldn't stand for it, Salt II or no Salt II. "Yanks or Ruskies," he'd said. "There's no blinkin' difference. They won't be satisfied 'til they've carved up the world between them." Mam told him not to be so daft, but we went down anyway. Granddad, Mam and me. Mam said Granddad didn't give her any choice.

Mam said Granddad bought the shelter in 1962 – during the Cuban Crisis. Ordered it through a Swedish catalogue. It had everything. Bomb-proof doors, ventilation equipment, a water store and recycling unit, bathroom fitments, disposal unit – and a two-ring cooker. Mam and Grandma were sworn to secrecy. None of the neighbours in Colliery Terrace had to know about it.

Mam said Granddad made a lot of mess and noise putting it in. Grandma was worried about what the neighbours would say.

"What we do in this house is our own business," Granddad had said. "So if that old nosy parker next door asks, just tell her we're putting in a sauna in the cellar. Nothing else, mind. Once they know what we've got, there'll be no keeping them out when the balloon goes up."

Granddad spent all his spare time in the cellar. Mam said there was a lot of gossip about his 'renovation' work after Grandma left. The police came round. Said the neighbours were worried. They didn't know Grandma had got fed up and run off with a brush salesman. Mind, she wasn't a Grandma then of course. She was forty-something, and Mam was only thirteen. After the police incident, Mam said Granddad never spoke to any of the neighbours again.

Granddad retired in 1967 because of his cough. He was only fifty then. The Management didn't like men with coughs in the pit. He didn't mind. It gave him more time for the shelter. He made lists of everything – right down to the last bar of soap. He'd even worked out what was needed for a basic diet of 1900 calories a day – 200 calories above the basal metabolic rate to sustain health in a low-activity environment over long periods. He told me that.

Then he started making modifications. Mam said he spent days in the library. Something to do with the electrics and the amount of energy used heating water to boiling point. He strengthened the racking and bought twelve car batteries – the lifetime guarantee sort – from different garages, and an alternator. He wired everything up to a second-hand Raleigh 12-speed racing bike he'd mounted on a stand and said an hour a day's pedalling should do it. He also bought three sizes of Thermos flask to save hot water.

Then he started stocking up on dried food. All sorts. You name it, he'd thought of it.

He bought it a bit at a time, so no one would think he was hoarding. It took up a lot of space down there, even with careful packing. Once Mam complained about it and Granddad said, "There'll be too much space when it's all gone. You just think about that."

Mam never liked the shelter. Said it was too small and too hot. I didn't mind. It was bigger than my bedroom.

I played in my bedroom a lot. Mam told me Granddad never wanted me to play out with other kids. Said they'd call me horrible names. "It's better he plays in the back yard on his own," he'd said. So that's what I did. Played in the yard or up in my room if it rained. I liked my room best. I felt safe in it.

Mam took me out once when Granddad was on one of his shopping trips. "It's not right for a little lad to be shut up all the time," she'd said. She took me down to the park to show me the ducks. I was really frightened. There was so much space and nowhere to hide. I screamed and screamed 'til we got back home. She never took me out again. I was glad about that.

Mam said Granddad burnt all our clothes in the yard one afternoon. "Pyjamas is all we'll need down there, my lass. Six pairs apiece for us and two pairs of three sizes for the lad. He can share mine when he's grown."

"I don't like wearing pyjamas, Dad," Mam had said.

"Well you won't need your fancy what-nots down there, my lass. I'm not Terry Hargreaves."

47

Conversations between Mam and Granddad always stopped when Terry Hargreaves was mentioned. I only asked about him once and Granddad cuffed me round the ear. That was the only time he ever lifted a finger to me.

Then there were the books Mam liked. Mills and Boon.

"You're not taking that rubbish, Ruby Warburton. You can read the Old Testament if you want to stuff your head with romantic drivel. David and Bathsheba. That should suit you."

"What's wrong with a bit of happiness-ever-after, Dad? I can't go down there knowing what's happening to everyone else up here without having something to – you know. It'd drive me daft."

"Then it'll have to drive you daft, my lass, because I'm not having that rubbish in *my* shelter."

So we took the Bible, the fourteen volumes of *Chambers's Encyclopaedia* (1961 edition) and its index, *Pears Cyclopaedia* (1978 edition), the *Concise Oxford Dictionary*, *Teach Yourself Mathematics*, *Russian for Beginners* (with two cassettes and a tape recorder), Scrabble, *A Treasury of Bedtime Stories and Nursery Rhymes*, Palgrave's *Golden Treasury and Additional Poems*, and of course the Diary.

He wouldn't take the *Pictorial Home Doctor*. "What can't be cured by a couple of aspirin, can't be cured," he said. So we took forty packets of assorted elastoplasts, three bottles of Dettol, four tubes of burn cream and thirty bottles of aspirin instead.

Granddad said he'd educate me. He'd got a stack of paper off-cuts from the printing works and bought 250 HB pencils,

12 rubbers, 25 packs of multi-coloured crayons, a large pot of school glue and a geometry set. He also got me a plastic school recorder and instruction book.

Mam took a few things she kept hidden in a large toilet bag locked in the medicine cabinet. When Granddad told her about the recorder, she took some earplugs as well.

Granddad took ten crossword books, his cut-throat razor kit, the old mandolin and a pack of cards.

Besides Teddy, Granddad said I could have a ball of string and the little snow scene in a plastic bottle – but not the elastic bands. He said they might get into places they shouldn't.

So on New Year's Eve 1979 Granddad left a note for the milkman. 'Emigrated'. I held Mam's hand and we went down the cellar steps in our pyjamas – mine were blue, hers were yellow and Granddad's stripy – and closed the shock-proof doors behind us.

Granddad started the Diary on the first of January 1980. It was the five-year sort. Thick, with a blue leather binding and gold at the edges. He ruled a line across the middle of each page to make it last ten years.

I didn't mind the shelter then. It was warm and I liked the sound of the ventilation fan. At night the toilet would make funny gurgling noises like my tummy. Teddy and I used to giggle about it under the covers. After a while I didn't notice them any more. Funny how you get used to things. Even Granddad snoring.

Mam slept in the camp bed next to me. After my eighth birthday, she hung a spare sheet between us from the pipes on the ceiling, like the one between her and Granddad.

We had a regular routine every day for five years. Granddad would set the alarm for 7.30 and we'd take it in turns to use the bathroom. I was last, so I got an extra half-hour in bed.

Mam did breakfast while I was washing. I thought the dried milk was much nicer than the watery stuff the milkman used to leave. It made the porridge taste really good.

After breakfast Mam cleared up and Granddad tidied the beds. I used to help him. "That's what they teach you in the army, my lad," he would say. "Discipline. A tidy man has a tidy mind."

Then we'd unfold the card table and sun-chairs and start lessons. Mam had to join in. She hated it.

"It's no good adopting that attitude, my lass. He's your lad and if anything happens to me, he's your responsibility. So you'd better know where he's up to with his studies."

I remember Mam got angry. "You're a bloody old fool, Fred Warburton! You don't even know if World War Three's going to happen – and you've got us down here like sardines in a bloody tin can!"

Granddad went a funny purple colour. "You just watch your language in front of the lad, Ruby. I don't know where you picked it up from – but I can guess – same place you picked up something else no doubt." And he looked at me. "Now sit down and we'll teach the lad the alphabet."

I liked alphabet days best. We'd tip out all the Scrabble tiles and play games until dinner time at 12.30. Once I could read, we used the Cyclopaedia for history, geography and science, and when I was nine, Granddad said I was old enough to start on Volume 1 of the *Encyclopaedia*. I felt really grown-up.

Mam got off the last half-hour of morning lessons so she could make the dinner. It was usually soup and mash. If I guessed the right flavour I could have an extra dried apricot afterwards.

After dinner Granddad would have a snooze. Mam would do some washing or mending and I was allowed one sheet of paper to draw on. I used to copy the drawings out of the nursery rhyme book at first. When I got older I used to draw things out of my head or make patterns with the compass. If they were any good, Granddad would let me stick them on the back of the shock-proof door. There wasn't any room on the walls. The pipes and food racks always got in the way.

At 3.30 Granddad would get up and spend half-an-hour on the bike recharging the batteries. Mam took over when he got out of breath. She used to sit pedalling furiously, staring at the wall. Granddad said I could do his turn for him when I got older. I was too small at first but by the time I was nine my feet reached the pedals.

At 4.00, we would have another hour-and-a-half of lessons, usually maths, and Mam would make tea using the hot water she'd stored in the thermos. I liked the apple puree and custard best.

After tea Granddad would play his mandolin and sing while Mam cleared up. He had a good voice for a man with a cough. When I was eight and my hands got a bit bigger, he began to teach me how to play the recorder. I wasn't very good at it but I got better. Sometimes we'd play a duet. Mam used to go into the bathroom and stay there until we'd finished. She said she was learning Russian.

We all had a drink of hot chocolate at 8.00 and then Granddad would bring out the Diary from under his bed. "Right," he'd say. "Let's see if we can remember everything we've done today. Everything, mind."

Some days were the same as the one before, except I'd have learnt something new, of course. But there were really big events like when I could say the alphabet on my own, or count up to a thousand. Then there was the great day when I actually finished Volume 1 of the *Encyclopaedia*, A – AUT. 21st June 1984.

I remember two other really big events. 18th December 1980 – and 31st December 1984. December seems to have been a momentous month in my life.

Just before our first Christmas we were putting up the decorations we'd made out of string and cut-up soup packets when there was a horrible thud. All the pipes rattled and the air pump gulped twice. We all stood stock still and listened.

"They've dropped it," Granddad said very quietly. "They've finally dropped it." There were tears in his eyes.

Mam just stared at the ceiling, eyes like black blobs in her face. Then she began to shake. Granddad put his arms around her and leaned her head on his shoulder. That was the only time I ever remember him doing that. "It's all right, Ruby. It's just ground shock coming through the absorbers."

He beckoned me over and we stood in the middle of the

shelter in our pyjamas, hugging each other, listening to the house crashing down above us. Bits of it kept on crashing down all afternoon, and then it all went very quiet.

That evening Granddad wrote in the Diary, "18th December – At 1.30 the Bomb dropped. Shelter seems undamaged. Air filters seem to be working. No radiation registering on the Geiger. Will know tomorrow if ventilation system is all right or not.".

Mam asked how he would know. Granddad mumbled something about we'd all know soon enough if it wasn't.

After the bomb, Mam got edgier. She bit her nails and spent longer in the bathroom. Sometimes when we spoke to her, she didn't hear us. She seemed to be listening for something else. She started talking to herself a lot too – especially when she was doing her stint on the bike.

"There might be people still alive up there," she said one evening when she was pedalling.

"Don't talk so daft. The air blast and heat radiation'll've wiped the place clean for miles."

Mam wasn't convinced. She still listened, sometimes for hours on end. Sometimes, she would just sing to herself. Her favourite was 'Yesterday'. I liked this. She had a nice voice. Granddad hated it. Said she shouldn't sing such drivel. It was bad for morale.

Granddad liked stirring songs. 'Keep Right on to the End of the Road' and 'Pack up your Troubles in your Old Kit Bag'. We'd play a duet together, him singing fit to burst. For an encore, we'd do 'It's a Long Way to Tipperary'.

Mam used to hate it. "You're a bloody sham, Fred

Warburton," she screamed at him one evening. "You weren't even in the bloody Army. They wouldn't have you!"

Granddad got up very slowly and drew himself up to his full height of five-foot-six. I remember his face went very red and his eyes bulged. "For your information, my lass, miners were key workers – and proud of it. *We* fought the war underground. Down there in the filth and dust. Sweating. Coughing. We didn't think of the dangers. It was up to us to keep the steel works and power stations going."

"Like 1974, I suppose."

Whenever Mam was having a bad time, she always brought up 1974. Something to do with a three-day week and power cuts.

"It wouldn't have happened if the electric hadn't gone off," I remember her complaining once when she thought I was asleep. "We were only trying to keep warm."

Granddad snorted. "You must think your old Dad was born yesterday, my lass. Next you'll be telling me you're the reincarnation of the Virgin Mary and Terry Hargreaves was the Archangel Gabriel."

"He would've married me if you hadn't shown him the door!"

"And where would you be now, my lass, eh? Up there. Fried to a crisp, along with your fancy fella and young Nigel."

"It might've been better than this. Sitting down here like moles waiting for God-knows-what to happen. I don't care what's up there! I want to get out!"

"You'll stop being so damned selfish, my lass, and think

of your responsibility to that lad. You owe him something after giving him such a bad start. You think about that."

She thought about it. I could tell. She used to stare at the door when Granddad was asleep and bite her nails. When he was awake, she would take *Russian for Beginners* and lock herself in the bathroom. I could hear her muttering to herself.

I suppose what happened was all my fault. I didn't mean to cause trouble. I was just curious. It was just after Christmas 1984 and Granddad was getting excited about starting page one of the Diary again in three days' time and talking about what we'd be doing for the next five years. Mam was staring at the door again. I wanted to go to the toilet. When I went into the bathroom I found her toilet bag on the shelf. She usually kept it locked away. I opened it.

"Look what I've found, Granddad."

I don't think I'll ever forget their faces. Hers went really white. His went the colour of the plums in the picture of Little Jack Horner.

"Give them to me, lad!"

"No!" Mam screamed. "They're mine! They're mine!" She snatched at the books I was holding and they fell on the floor. I remember the pages flip-flopping when they landed.

Granddad picked them up slowly and read the covers. Then he took a deep breath and went over to the saucepan cupboard. Mam just watched him. He got out the big saucepan, filled it with water and began ripping out the pages and pushing them into the pan.

"Waste not, want not," he said. "When I said there was

no room down here for this rubbish, my lass, I meant it. But we'll not waste the paper, will we Nigel? It'll make papier-mâché for you to do some modelling." And he kept on stuffing the pages into the pan.

Mam never gave me a goodnight kiss after that. I still cry when I think about it.

On New Year's Eve, she must've dosed our hot chocolate while we were writing the Diary.

We didn't hear the alarm the next morning. It was after 9.00 when we woke up and found she'd gone. She'd taken the *Russian for Beginners* book. I couldn't get the hang of it without the book so I gave up in the end.

When Granddad realised what she'd done he used a lot of language I'd never heard before, but I don't think it was Russian. He kept checking the Geiger counter. I thought it best to keep out of his way so I made breakfast. By the time I'd finished, he seemed to have calmed down. The porridge wasn't all that good but I got better with practice.

When we were eating, Granddad looked at me and said in his very serious voice, "She could have killed us, you know, doing that. No sense of responsibility, that was her problem. Always was. Just like her mother."

So we started 1985 without her. I missed her a lot. I even got Teddy out from the spare bedding box and took him to bed with me again for a few months. I hadn't needed him for ages.

I think Granddad missed her too. Only he wasn't going to say so. He took down her bed and stacked it behind the assorted dried fruit cartons. Then he put the card table and chairs in the space that was left. By mid-June, it was hard to remember what she looked like. Just a white blur with black blobs for eyes.

I wasn't very good at doing her sort of things at first. The buttons I sewed on always fell off. Granddad couldn't sew at all. His cooking wasn't all that good either. He kept getting the amounts all wrong. So I started doing the cooking as well. I had to wash the pyjamas too. His hands were getting too knobbly at the knuckles. They hurt him when he tried to wring out the water.

Doing all the chores meant there wasn't much time for anything else except lessons, and sometimes Granddad's after-dinner doze lasted until tea-time. If I got into an interesting topic, like Diseases of the Endocrine System or European Culture in the Lower Palaeolithic Period, things didn't get done. That's how we almost let the batteries run down.

I remember it was 19th August 1988. I got bogged down with the theoretical significance of magnetostriction the day before, and forgot to do the afternoon stint. In the evening I'd wanted to finish Volume 8 J – MAJ before chocolate time. Granddad wasn't feeling up to doing his bit and I'd forgotten I'd only done half-an-hour in the morning because there was some washing to do. The lights started to go dim before I remembered. We turned off everything except the ventilation fan and I pedalled like blazes for a solid hour. I was shattered. Granddad was really cross.

"Discipline, lad. Discipline. You can't afford to let things slip."

I don't think I noticed Granddad was getting old 'til one morning in November 1988. I was fourteen. He was seventy-one. He had trouble getting out of bed. He said his legs were aching. I gave him a couple of aspirin, breakfast in bed and shaved him. When he fell asleep again I did a stint on the bike. I managed twenty-five mph for fifteen minutes. It made me hungry so I ate the porridge he'd left and made another plateful. We still had masses of the stuff.

Granddad was shrinking. I thought at first it was just me getting taller. But it wasn't. His pyjamas started to hang off his shoulders and fall off his hips. We kept them up with some of my string for a while. By April 1989, I was wearing his and he was wearing mine.

Our routines started going to pieces after that. Granddad had to keep going back to bed. He complained of pains in his legs and chest. He gave up singing. I gave him aspirins when he wanted them and kept him clean and fed. He slept a lot and I got on with my learning. I was just beginning Volume 11 POL – ROS.

By last Christmas, he didn't get up any more. I hung up the decorations on my own and made his favourite fruit and custard pudding.

On Christmas morning he said, "Don't you ever want to go up, lad? Go up and see what's left of the big wide world? See what happened to your mam?" It was the first time he'd mentioned her for years.

I didn't say anything. I'd never thought much about it.

On Boxing Day, I wrote the Diary for the first time. Granddad was too tired. I did my best writing. It wasn't copper-plate like his, but I didn't make any mistakes and I know he was proud of me.

He liked me to read to him. I'd spend hours sitting by his bed going through what we'd done on a particular day. He would lie there with a smile on his face, nodding when he wanted more. I never read him the bits I knew would upset him. Like Mam leaving.

I was just finishing writing the last entry on New Year's Eve when he made a strange gurgling sort of noise. I bent over to see if he needed anything. His eyes were staring at the ceiling.

I suppose I knew he was dead. It was just I didn't really want to think about it. I closed his eyes and sat on the bed the whole night wondering what to do. I couldn't think of a single thing except *waste not, want not*.

Next morning was the same. I left him on the bed, made breakfast, tidied up and came back to sitting on the bed wondering what to do. I only just remembered to do my stint on the bike. I thought it might help me think of something. I suppose it did – eventually. I was getting up to twenty-five mph on 7th January when I remembered *if in doubt, look it up*. That's when I read up **Dead, Disposal of the** in Volume 4 CON – EDU and the bit about living with putrefying corpses being unhygienic.

Once I'd put the last chunk of him into the waste disposal unit, I put the hacksaw away and washed the floor, folded up his bedding and packed it in an empty box we used for storing the dried sultanas. I was glad I could make use of the carton because I hadn't been able to think of anything useful to do with it up 'til then.

I took down his bed and stacked it next to Mum's behind
the rest of the dried fruit boxes. After I'd cleared his bed
away it felt really spooky – like I said.

I started hearing noises at night. Sometimes they'd wake
me up and I'd get goose bumps all down my arms. I'd put
my light on and when I knew it was safe, I'd get Teddy and
take him back to bed with me. Then the air pump started
acting up and making a whining sort of noise every now
and then. What with that and the disposal unit going wonky,
I got scared.

So that's why I came up.

Sorry about messing up your rose bed. I didn't expect it
to be there, you see. I thought there'd be ruins and things
– and what was left of 32 Colliery Terrace. It was a bit of
a shock when all that soil and horse muck fell in on me.

No, I didn't know about the demolition order or the Council's Urban Redevelopment and Open Spaces Programme.
But the ventilation pipe looks quite nice with that little statue
thing on top of it. Granddad would've liked that.

Do you think the woman and that little girl will be all
right? They wouldn't stop screaming. I couldn't help running
around and yelling like that. Honest. Parks frighten me.
There's so much space and nowhere to hide.

Thanks for rescuing me. It was a dog, wasn't it? That
black thing that made a lot of noise and kept jumping up
at me? It tried to grab Teddy.

I like your house, by the way. Oh, it's a hut. Well anyway,
it's nice and warm. It's cold outside – specially in pyjamas.
I'd forgotten what cold felt like. Daylight's darker than I

expected too. And the air smells all funny. Can't describe it. Perhaps it's the manure.

I should've thanked you for the tea. Sorry, I forgot. *Chashka chay-yoo*. A cup of tea. That's all I remember in Russian. I'm glad you're not Russian. I wouldn't have got very far with just *chashka chay-yoo*, would I?

I don't suppose you know what happened to Mam, do you? No, well it was five years ago. And it was New Year's Eve. Granddad used to say people got dressed up on New Year's Eve and acted a bit daft. Probably nobody noticed her in muddy yellow pyjamas. These are Granddad's of course. Stripy. They were clean on yesterday. Not that you'd notice now with all this muck on them.

Pity about the Diary. I must've I dropped it when all that soil and stuff fell on my head. Granddad would be cross if he knew. *Waste not, want not*, he used to say.

SUCH STUFF AS DREAMS ARE MADE ON

It had rained all night: heavy summer rain that streamed down like continuous strands of cellophane from a leaden sky. Dawn was reluctant to break, ignoring the summons of the City Hall clock which had just struck five with funereal solemnity. Conscious of the time, the street lights flickered and extinguished themselves, leaving the deserted boulevards awash with streaks of silver grey.

Fifty floors up in the darkened Artco building, Carlton Munro had a headache. One of many. Half dressed and unkempt, he lay on his back, sprawled out like a discarded doll on the cracking black leather couch in the corner of his studio. Somewhat dramatically, he had flung an arm across his face, defending his eyes from the non-existent light. On the floor within easy groping distance, even with his eyes closed, was a supply of whisky bottles – most of them empty – silent witnesses to the sudden paucity of his inspiration.

For ten years it had been so easy: too easy. Ideas had sprung up like magic beanstalks overnight, blossomed and flourished. Comic-strip heroes by the dozen. No more. Times had changed.

Munro remembered. Through the insistent beating at his temples, he could recall the precise event which triggered his irreversible decline: Ponsonby's retirement and the arrival of Winthrop. Winthrop – Editor-in-Chief. Five hellish years of him. Winthrop, who made pronouncements over the phone, never face-to-face; Winthrop, who was such a stickler for deadlines; Winthrop, the enthusiastic new broom out to make changes.

No more heroes, Winthrop decreed: villains were in. Villains were what kids really wanted these days. Blood and guts and plenty of it.

Munro had loved his heroes: Thorswain and Sharma; Philobar and Chantra. He had lavished care and attention on them. Love even. His villains had been bit-players, tools, a means to an end, the objects of derring-do – nothing more.

Times had changed. Winthrop wanted 'whiz-bangers', as he called them, his piping voice crackling with enthusiasm down the phone. Grotesque monsters. The more grotesque, the more Winthrop loved them. Quumvorg from the Slime. Artraxis – Eater of the Dead. Hagarblast the Unspeakable Horror. Grindorahl...Munro's head throbbed. Each mutation more repulsive, more repellent than the last. The stuff of nightmares.

The more grotesque, the less easily Munro could conjure them up – not without a tot of whisky here and there to fire his imagination. The tot had become a bottle, and then another bottle, and then several. His consumption had begun to exceed his income. And still Winthrop wanted more.

"The kids love 'em," Winthrop would pipe at him from the other end of the line at some ungodly hour in the night, waking Munro from his alcoholic stupor to enthuse on his latest creations. "Give 'em more!"

Munro had been running on alcohol ever since. It kept him balanced on that fine knife-edge dividing reality from illusion, wakefulness from dreaming. It kept him working. It kept him meeting Winthrop's deadlines. Until now.

Munro pressed his arm closer to his eyes, blocking out the world: his world.

In the Stygian gloom of the alcove opposite stood his work-desk, mocking him, smothered in a rag-bag mountain of discarded scribblings, a further testimony, if any were needed, to the sudden dislocation of his thought processes. Papers everywhere. Jumbled. Dumped. Ditched. The dung heap of a detached brain. Winthrop wanted action and Munro was empty, his brain a perfect void. And all because of Vraakenstraag.

...Vraakenstraag.

Vraakenstraag, the Soul-Snatcher, the Consumer of Existence. Vraakenstraag the Omnipotent who, despite copious quantities of fire-water on Munro's part, had steadfastly refused to solidify into a 'whiz-banger'. Vraakenstraag persisted as an insubstantial incubus, a formless entity in Munro's brain with the exception of one solitary feature – a single, glowing, iridescent, hypnotic eye.

Munro's arm developed pins and needles. Painfully, he lowered it and eased himself into a sitting position, carefully manoeuvring his legs off the couch. His feet touched the ground and knocked over an empty bottle in the process. He heard it teeter, collapse and roll away across the carpetless floor coming to rest with an audible clunk against the side of the desk. The sound echoed and re-echoed in his brain with an agonising intensity. He held his head in his hands and cursed softly under his breath, the blood at his temples drumming on unmercifully. He sat immobile for a moment and waited for the pain to lessen. It didn't.

Beyond the drumming, he heard something else. A soft rustling. It came from the depths of the darkened alcove beside his desk as though a faint wind had stirred the long dead leaves of winter. He lifted his head slowly, uncertain, squinting hopelessly into the gloom across a thin shaft of weak daylight stabbing downwards through the window blinds onto the floor.

In the half-light beyond, he thought he could see a dim outline: the back of a dark, hooded shape hunched over his desk rifling softly through his papers with a curious deliberation.

Munro's outrage surfaced above his stupor. "What the hell do you think you're doing?" he croaked, struggling unsteadily to his feet.

The shape bending over the desk turned slowly, pulling back into the shadows. "Looking for your new creation," replied the strangely familiar voice reminiscent of so many late night phone calls.

Munro's brow furrowed, his brain wrestling with confusion. "Winthrop?" he asked, bewildered.

"I thought it was time I paid you a visit. Time for us to meet."

"What do you want?" Munro demanded, fighting hard to remain upright on his feet.

"The deadline was yesterday," Winthrop's piping voice reminded him. "You promised me a new creation, Munro. You've let me down." He sounded hurt, almost peevish. "It's only half finished. That really isn't good enough."

Munro could feel sweat breaking out on his forehead and in the stubble on his upper lip. "Look Winthrop, give me a couple more days. It's nearly there. Just give me a couple more days."

"I can't wait that long, I'm afraid. Deadlines have to be met. You know that."

Munro gulped, the droplets of sweat coalescing into rivulets tracking their way down his face and neck. He stumbled forward, pleading for time, tripped and fell headlong onto the floor. For a moment he saw blackness, then stars, unfocussed stars, pin-pricks of light dancing in the glass of the errant whisky bottle perilously close to his face. He groaned and rolled over, staring up into the hooded face of his tormentor leaning over him.

At first he saw the smile: a broad, face-splitting smile that left his stomach crawling with fear. And then he no longer cared: his gaze was fixed elsewhere – on a point a little way above the reptilian jawline – on the pulsating brightness that had begun to throb remorselessly, exquisitely, from the depths of a glowing, single, iridescent eye.

LEST WE FORGET

It was almost the eleventh hour of the eleventh day of the eleventh month.

We stood with the crowd in the thin November air wearing our poppies, feeling cold and light-headed. Our eyes blinked against the piercing glare of the winter sun flooding out from behind the stark silhouette of the cenotaph which rose up solid and menacing before us.

Ahead of us through a gap in the crowd, I could see the Queen walking forward to take her place. Diminutive, sombrely dressed, and with the same grit and determination of her great-grandmother, she turned to face the full brilliance of the low-slanting sun.

The background hum of conversation died away to stillness, everyone waiting for the great well of silence that would follow the striking of the hour.

I cast a quick glance across Whitehall to where the Veterans' representatives stood, and felt a small stab of pride as I picked out the figure of my father, standing tall despite his advancing years, his medals glinting in the morning light. From under his peaked cap his eyes looked straight ahead, fixed on the monolith before him. He knew what it was to be brave in the face of danger.

Automatically, my eyes scanned the rooftops. I knew where to look. Behind balustrades and in strategic window openings, the dark shapes of police marksmen were poised: waiting; watching; ready to react if they were needed. Even though it no longer mattered in my case, their presence reassured me.

Standing to my right, my son, Damien, seventeen and showing increasing signs of rebellion in our father-son relationship, was shuffling his feet and whispering something to Gemma, his younger sister. I nudged him with my elbow. He glared at me. "How much longer, Dad?" he said through gritted teeth. "I'm frozen."

I'd no time to reply. The hour began to strike, the hugeness of the sound washing over the assembled crowds like a tidal wave, moving on and leaving silence in its wake.

There is something eerie in the silence of a multitude. When I was Damien's age, I was only dimly aware of it. Since Lydia's death however, it's grown much stronger. I recognise it now as the silence of individual grief and remembrance coalescing into a single overwhelming sense of loss, all the more potent because it's so much greater than the sum of all its many parts.

Every year for me, those precious seconds of straining emptiness that follow the tolling of the eleventh hour, are as much about remembering Lydia as all those who've died in so many human conflicts over time.

In the early years after her death, I tried to hide the emotion this tide of silence conjured up in me. But in the last few years, I've unashamedly let the tears flow, perhaps because I've learned to let go of my fear. I know my weakness, as they see it, embarrasses my children, but if it shows them the grief of mortal loss, then later in their own lives perhaps they'll come to their own understanding of what it means to lose someone that they love.

With brimming eyes, I ignored Damien's half-glance in my direction, and kept my gaze on my father. His face was impassive.

I can only marvel at this fortitude. As a much younger man on active service, he saw so many of his dearest friends killed or injured, caught in deadly crossfire or the blast from a hidden device. Yet he can still stand dry-eyed and tight-lipped, disciplined and erect, while his son mourns the loss of a wife killed after a geological field trip that went horribly wrong.

The minute passed. The guns boomed out their tribute, the echo startling a group of feeding pigeons and starlings, sending them fluttering upwards into the china-blue canopy of the sky above the grey buildings.

The buglers in their immaculate dress uniforms sounded 'Reveille'. The tension eased, and a few spectators dabbed at their eyes, as I did mine.

The Queen accepted the large wreath from her equerry and walked forward to pay homage to the fallen. Her head bowed briefly in acknowledgement before the monument before she turned and retraced her steps to her allotted place looking composed and contemplative. Perhaps she was thinking of her brother.

I scanned the rooftops again. The watchers remained vigilant.

The edge to the wind suddenly seemed much colder. A sudden gust stirred the remnants of the frosted leaves still clinging to the plane trees, snatching them up and sending them tumbling to the ground. Several fell around my father. He was still standing to attention, waiting his turn to place his wreath on behalf of the Veterans. He remained unmoving; patient – a soldier performing his duty.

Damien was shuffling his feet again, pulling a face to show the full extent of his irritation. "I'm bloody cold," he muttered, hunching up inside his coat.

I lost my temper and heard him swear under his breath in response, loud enough to be heard by two elderly ladies in front of him. They turned and glared at us both.

I don't know who was more embarrassed – the son or the father.

The military band struck up a stirring march and the effect on my father was electrifying. His chin came up, and with a stride that would have been the envy of a man half his years, he strode forward, saluting crisply as he handed over his wreath to an attendant, and marched on with his comrades in time to the music. In that moment, I felt my pride leap forward, striding off with him as he marched into the distance.

The dark shapes on the rooftops and in the windows watched it all.

Once the parade began to move off, I sensed keeping Damien under control much longer would be a lost cause.

I stifled my irritation aware that Gemma was cold too – except she hadn't complained. I suggested we go to an eatery a couple of streets away, and they could order what they wanted to warm themselves. Damien, hands buried deep inside his coat pockets muttered something along the lines of, "About bloody time, too," which I pretended not to hear, and we set off, part of the crowd melting away into the side-streets.

Gemma sat next to me, hugging her mug and sipping the steaming hot chocolate with care. "Will we be able to see Grandpa before we leave?" she asked.

I shook my head. "He said he'd feel happier if we fixed our flight plans and got away without trying to meet up after the Veterans' Reunion."

Gemma looked crestfallen. "When will we see him again?" she asked.

"It depends when I can get leave. Rosters are rosters. I can't take precedence every time."

She frowned at the implications of this with all the seriousness of a fifteen-year-old going on sixteen. "I hope it won't be too long," she said, adding because the thought clearly worried her, "They'll let us come back for his centenary in July, won't they?"

"I'll get special leave for that," I assured her.

Damien, sitting opposite us and still sulking, said nothing. I'd ignored him up to now, hoping he'd snap out of it. But it looked like he wasn't going to this time around.

Over the last couple of months there'd been a series of little incidents like this, but he'd always pulled himself together before I'd felt the need to make an issue of it. Today, however, he was being unusually stubborn.

"What's the matter with *you*?" I asked bluntly, provoked more than usual by his behaviour, so that the words came out sharper than I'd intended.

He looked me straight in the eye. "I'm not coming here again next year," he said defiantly.

I suppose every father has this moment. Independence Day. I don't know what I expected would happen, but he'd finally chosen to defy me over the one thing I was least likely to give way on. I could feel my anger boiling up inside.

Gemma touched my arm. "Damien doesn't understand," she said simply.

He glared across at her, her collusion with me over his defection more than he could bear. All his truculence was suddenly channelled in her direction. "Don't I?" he snapped. "This bloody charade's all about Dad and his bloody hang-ups, isn't it? Not Grandpa. Every year he drags us back here – hanging about for hours – getting bloody cold. I'm sick of it!" He stood up suddenly, and with a dramatic gesture, snatched the poppy from his lapel. "This is meaningless," he said, and threw it onto the floor.

He should never have done that – and he knew it. I could tell from the sudden panicky look in his eyes. It gave me the upper hand. "Pick that up!" I commanded in the voice I used when addressing subordinates. Heads turned at the tables around us. People stopped talking.

"No!" he countered, my attempt to reassert my dominance over him refuelling his rebellion.

"Pick it up!" I said, rising to my feet, my anger blazing in my head.

"No!"

We could have come to blows. We were shouting at one another across the space of a small table, making an unedifying spectacle of ourselves.

Gemma, to her eternal credit, quietly got off her stool and picked up the poppy. She twirled it in her fingers and thrust it between our faces, the blood-red petals a challenge to our antagonism. "This isn't meaningless," she said very softly, still twirling the poppy in front of our eyes. "It's a reminder of what stupidity and arrogance can lead to."

Damien blushed almost as scarlet as the petals of the flower. From the heat rushing up from under my collar, no doubt I did the same.

"If we forget the millions of people who died in the past," she went on, addressing us like a mother chiding a pair of wilful children, "it'll be that much easier to let millions die in the future, won't it?" And she placed the poppy back under its pin on his lapel.

In the face of her lecture we both subsided into a humbled, embarrassed silence. We shuffled back onto our seats and those around us turned away and resumed their interrupted conversations. After a while, we were grateful to slip back into our previous anonymity.

We ate the rest of the meal in silence and afterwards Damien, keen to absent himself as soon as he could, made the excuse he'd arranged to meet up with some old friends for the afternoon. I didn't remind him of our flight time home – or to watch his back: that would have added insult to injury.

Outside, in the crisp afternoon air with long shadows stabbing the pavements, I scanned the street with a practised eye. Nothing.

Gemma was hanging onto my arm, keeping close. "Daddy," she said suddenly, looking up at me. "I think we should go to the art gallery – like you used to – with Mummy. Don't you think we should?"

She didn't have to say it – that not all the casualties of war die on the battlefield. Others have a less glorious end and no cenotaph to mark their passing. Hostages rarely make it home. Rescues have a notoriously high failure rate. It's always a gamble – a gamble I'd been prepared to take. Afterwards, I'd time enough to reflect on what we could have done better – or differently – given the limited options we had on the table. A pointless exercise, better not pursued – but I'd pursued it anyway, dissecting every minute detail as if this might somehow help turn back the clock and our lives could go on just the same as before. Except they couldn't.

I nodded. It seemed the right thing to do. "I'll call a cab," I said.

"No – let's walk," she insisted, tilting her head slightly in that defiant way of hers I'd grown to cherish. She was smiling: confident; a capable young woman who could handle almost anything. The little girl who'd been hanging onto my arm had disappeared. Instead, I was looking into a face that had suddenly taken on so many of Lydia's mature features. The transformation almost winded me and left a palpable pain around my heart. "It's nice to feel the wind in your face," she was saying. "Even if it's cold."

I gave in as graciously as I could and we set off at a brisk pace, arm-in-arm, keeping in step as we marched along. The streets were strangely quiet after all the hustle and bustle of the morning. There were a few people, like ourselves, hurrying along the pavements eager to reach their destinations out of the cold, but that was all.

I was suddenly struck by a terrible thought, probably brought on by the unsettling incident with Damien. "Do you really think people will go on remembering, Gemma?" I asked. "Once your Grandpa's generation's gone?

"We still have soldiers, Daddy," she reminded me.

"Yes, but not wars – not wars like there used to be."

"Maybe not," she conceded after a moment's reflection. "We have 'hostilities' instead, don't we?"

I couldn't help smiling: she'd hit upon the dishonesty embedded in the language that everyone adopted. 'War' was a taboo three-letter word: too short and brutal, conjuring up the unacceptable. Better to mask the hideousness and wanton waste of human life in terminology that could just as easily describe a playground fracas. But it begged the question – "Does it matter what we call them?" I asked.

"Probably not."

"Do you think there'll ever be a time when we don't have wars? – whatever we call them?"

She stopped and turned to confront me, a ghost of a smile flickering briefly across her lovely face. "Who knows,

Daddy?" she said with a small, hopeless shrug. "There's always an excuse, isn't there? If it's not politics, it's religion. If it's not religion, it's something else. It just seems to be human nature, doesn't it? To fight?"

It was a rhetorical question, I realised, the unedifying scene over lunch confirming the uncomfortable truth of her observation.

"So you think we should still have a special day – like this – to remind us?"

She pondered on the value of this for a moment, then linking her arm into mine again, she began to lead me up the gallery steps. "I think it's better to remember than to forget," she said.

★ ★ ★

Like the rest of the passengers, I knew we would doze for most of the flight: it was a long-haul back. Already some of them had closed off their seating areas and turned down the lights. Damien was across the aisle, lying back, eyes tight shut, tuned into his favourite music. Next to me, Gemma was gazing out of the window, absorbing everything there was to see.

The events of the day had left me strangely troubled, wrestling with doubts and fears. There were times when Lydia's absence hurt more than usual. This was one of them. There were decisions to be made and I badly needed her infallible commonsense to make them.

I'd married late, all my energies channelled into annihilating the latest incarnation of the suicidal anarchist movement – the Freedom Army – a collection of misfit fanatics tearing our society apart. And then suddenly and unexpectedly I'd fallen in love – deeply in love. I was much older than she was, and it never entered my head I'd be the one to see our children become children no longer – that she'd not be with me to see this amazing, and often bewildering, transition.

That summer – fifteen years ago, when Gemma was little more than a baby – we'd got sound intelligence a resurgent cell was setting up down on the South Side. We'd learned from experience you had to crush these embryonic cankers in their infancy. We'd almost left it too late the first time round and they'd become difficult to eradicate – like the mythical Hydra. We'd no sooner lopped off one head than two more sprang up in its place.

I don't know why, but I guessed from the start I was their target. I'd had several warnings over the years and taken the necessary precautions. But when they couldn't reach me, they took Lydia instead – a softer target because she was too trusting of those around her. They shot her when their hideout was stormed, so I suppose you could say they achieved their aim – getting me out of the way. I resigned. Couldn't go on. Emigrated to the most secure location I could find and took Damien and Gemma with me. I did it with the best of intentions. But life moves on. I was of no interest to anyone now, I realised that, and Damien and Gemma were reaching an age when they needed to decide for themselves what they wanted from their future.

Gemma must have read my thoughts. She turned to look

at me and tried to smile. "Daddy," she said, not rushing things in case she hurt my feelings. "Maybe Damien and I have been away too long. Maybe we should go back down after we've finished our studies – sign up for peace-keeping with the UN." She hesitated, perhaps seeing the distress I felt written on my face. "What do you think?"

The hurt in my heart gripped me for a moment, then eased. I looked past her out of the window to where the Earth shone in the distance, a brilliant blue and white marbled disc set in the blackness of the heavens, and thought how beautiful and precious it was. They belonged there, not shut away in the claustrophobic security-fixated environment of the Station with its emergency drills and weekly defence-training sessions. I should let them go.

I didn't answer her immediately. My attention was diverted by a thin, balding man getting up from his seat a few rows in front of us. In no particular hurry, he made his way back along the cabin and stopped in the aisle next to me. There was something strangely familiar about him I couldn't place. He was smiling. A smile without humour. "Do you remember me, Mr Ryman?" he was asking as he unbuttoned his jacket and took out the gun. "We remember you," he added, pointing it straight at my head. "In fact – we never forget."

I felt Gemma's body stiffen slightly, like a coiled spring ready for action. Then she shot him.

CYPHER

Arthur couldn't say precisely when little rituals had become a big thing in his life. They'd sort of crept up on him, one by one. He could vaguely remember standing on a step-stool in front of the washbasin in the bathroom as a very young boy, grimacing into the shaving mirror and counting up to a hundred while he brushed his teeth. And he hadn't rushed the counting either. No, it had been slow and methodical. He didn't want to accidentally skip from fifty to sixty because he hadn't been concentrating. Concentration mattered. Even then, he realised, it was important to pay attention to what he was doing.

His father was 'slipshod' – or at least that's what he heard his mother say almost every day. "Harry Hepplewhite," she would say at the top of her voice, usually from the bottom of the stairs, "Can't you do *anything* right?" And his father would just shrug, like a duck throwing off water, and carry on up the stairs with his back turned resolutely towards her.

Arthur had no intention of growing up like his father and finding himself labelled 'slipshod'.

He'd had a hard time at school. Most of the kids in his year poked fun at him. He was an easy target. He was small, and thin. He liked order and precision. His books were just so in his desk; his pens and pencils where they should be in his pencil box, and his rubber always in the little place allocated to it next to the pencil sharpener. But he was never bullied. Maybe that was because he managed to maintain a low profile most of the time. He wasn't pushy or showy, like Jeremy Lightowler, always the first to put up his hand and answer a question, and as time passed, he harboured a sense of well-being from being undistinguished and indistinguishable.

His prowess on the playing field was equally unexceptional, his slight frame ensuring he was not the most obvious choice for any of the team games. And this situation was perfectly satisfactory as far as he was concerned. In this unassuming, unremarkable fashion, he made solid, steady progress through his school-days which occasionally got him noticed almost by accident as a 'reliable pupil'. His teachers, faced with his name on the end of term report, tended to restrict their comments to – "Arthur continues to work methodically and well, and is making steady progress," Arthur did not delude himself that this was in any way their fair or frank assessment of his capabilities. Most of them he knew, if they were honest, had considerable trouble trying to remember who he was.

At sixteen, he'd left school with average grades. Ambition to reach the top of any ladder wasn't what he had in mind. He knew precisely what he wanted – an undemanding job in an office where he could blend into the background and be left largely undisturbed to get on with whatever he had to do. He wanted to be nothing more than an unexceptional employee who was always there: solid and dependable; who'd turn up on time without fail; not ask for days off, and who'd clear his desk every evening by five-thirty sharp.

He was, as it turned out, just what Aitcheson & Aitcheson were looking for. Their offices were conspicuous and ostentatiously Georgian. Ionic columns framed the front entrance under a grandiose pediment at the top of a flight of polished granite steps. Access to the spacious atrium beyond, with its airy central staircase, was through a pair of half-glazed, highly varnished mahogany double doors, their brass-work gleaming and immaculate, courtesy of the daily attention lavished on them by William Pevensey, doorkeeper. These magnificent doors swung both ways on their hinges, closing with a satisfying *swish* behind everyone who came and went. They were a boon to anyone carrying heavy or bulky parcels. Opening them was a matter of applying a shoulder – or any other convenient part of the anatomy, as pert Polly Plumpton had once told Arthur, much to his embarrassment – and pushing.

It was these double doors that had impressed Arthur the most when he'd stood outside, fresh out of school in the new suit his mother had bought for him, and finally plucked up the courage to push open the right-hand one and step inside. It had *swished* shut behind him with a very positive *yessss* sound, giving Arthur the strong impression he'd somehow managed to pass muster, an impression reinforced half-an-hour later when he unexpectedly emerged as the new filing clerk starting the following Monday. Arthur had not actually applied for the post, he'd just turned up to see if there might be any vacancies. It just so happened that Mr Wrigglesworth, the Office Manager at the time, had been at a loss because Billy Billington had just told him where to stuff his job and walked out five minutes before never to be seen again.

"Are you any good at filing?" Mr Wrigglesworth had wanted to know. Arthur had honestly admitted he had no idea, but said he'd always got satisfaction from putting things in the right place – and that had been good enough as far as Mr Wrigglesworth was concerned.

So Arthur's life as part of Aitcheson & Aitcheson had begun.

And so had the little rituals. His daily routine, once established, became a habit he'd no wish to break: counting the number of paces from his parents' front gate to the bus stop; sitting in the third seat from the front of the bus on the right-hand side; counting the steps up to the front entrance; pushing open the right-hand door – always the right-hand door – never the left – into the spacious atrium with its parquet flooring, dado rail and panelling; nodding to Mr Pevensey reading his paper behind the front desk; counting down the steps into the basement to the filing room; keeping his head down to avoid any of the giggling typists he might meet on the way; acknowledging only Gladys, the tea-lady with her trolley, who always had a cheery "Morning, Arthur" for him.

There in the filing room, with its ten ranks of eight grey four-drawer filing cabinets, Arthur had been in his element.

Every morning out-trays brimming with invoices, copy letters and despatch notes would be left for his attention. He read every one of them, finding the right place for this piece of paper or that, until after several years, his knowledge of the intricate workings of Aitcheson & Aitcheson had reached encyclopaedic proportions. Not that anyone noticed, but Arthur thrived on having a profound sense of satisfaction in a job well done.

Then, unexpectedly, his life had changed. One Thursday morning, Mr Foggarty, one of the longest-serving members of staff, was found dead at his desk under a mountain of paperwork. Aitcheson & Aitcheson was in uproar. No one was entirely sure how long he'd been there but it could have been a day or two, the cleaners having long since given his office a wide berth.

Mr Wrigglesworth had spotted Arthur hovering on the edge of the curious crowd who'd watched the undertakers arrive to remove the corpse. "You – What's-his-name – you're in Filing aren't you?"

With all eyes turned on him, Arthur had had to confess he was.

"Go and sort out Mr Foggarty's desk during your lunch break, will you?" Mr Wrigglesworth had instructed him. "God knows what you'll find there. Do the best you can."

'Foggy', as Mr Foggarty had been dubbed by those less respectful members of staff, was as muddle-headed as it was possible to be without actually getting fired. He'd occupied an office round the corner at the far end of the long corridor on the top floor, an exalted domain Arthur had never had the temerity to explore. Mr Foggarty's existence, if not the rôle he actually fulfilled for Aitcheson & Aitcheson, was recognised by an old brass plate on the outside of his door which read simply 'Mr J Foggarty'.

When Arthur had thrown open the door and stood on the threshold, hardly daring to enter, he'd been greeted by the sight of heaps of files and assorted loose papers filling every conceivable space. They overflowed from the desk onto the floor around it, onto the tops of chairs and bookcases – even piling up onto the window sill – blocking out the light. For Arthur, it had been a joy to behold. A challenge. In fact, if he'd ever been asked – which no one did – he'd have said this had become the one burning ambition in his life – to clear Mr Foggarty's office of all its accumulated clutter.

For several months after Mr Foggarty's death, the old man's office – and its unloved paperwork – had remained untroubled by any sign of interest from Mr Wrigglesworth or anyone else. Without any instructions to the contrary, Arthur had continued to devote his solitary lunch breaks to the task of bringing order to chaos. Sitting behind Mr Foggarty's desk in Mr Foggarty's well-worn chair, he began to feel perfectly at home, as if the place had been waiting just for him.

Unhindered and unnoticed, he'd sifted through the mountain of paper, slowly at first, because he'd no idea what he was dealing with, except his encyclopaedic knowledge of Aitcheson & Aitcheson undoubtedly helped. He'd eventually got the hang of things and begun to return the papers and files to their rightful places in the Filing Room. He'd been on the point of mentioning this to Mr Wriggleswoth one day when Mr Aitcheson Senior had burst into the room and surveyed its changing state.

Mr Aitcheson Senior was a large, florid-faced man with a handlebar moustache and a voice not to be trifled with. "What are you doing here?" he'd demanded, and Arthur had floundered his way through an explanation mentioning Mr Wrigglesworth's instructions by the way.

Mr Aitcheson had frowned. "Think you could handle the job then?" he'd asked.

Arthur had said that he probably could.

"Right then – it's yours. What's your name again?"

Arthur had told him.

His name, engraved on a brass plate, had replaced Mr Foggarty's outside the door and remained there ever since.

With his change of duties, combined with the distinction of an office all to himself, Arthur's life slipped into a new and very different routine. He grew a moustache, and was suddenly addressed by all and sundry as "Mr Hepplewhite", an elevation which after six months or so led him to purchase a pin-striped suit, bowler hat and rolled umbrella. Mr Pevensey would nod respectfully when he came and went, to which Arthur would respond, "William," and tip his hat, and the giggling girls from the typing pool giggled no longer.

He now had several new rituals to incorporate into his daily life: the number of stairs to count from the atrium to the top floor, all forty-eight of them; the choice of turning right rather than turning left to reach his office; the number of paces along the corridor before the corner, and the equal number of paces to his door at the far end – fifty-six in total; not forgetting the ten doors on either side of the corridor leading into offices he never felt any need to enter as he passed them at eight-thirty sharp every morning and five-thirty every night.

The years passed and small changes crept into his life. At first it was minor matters on the home front: his father went out one night and never returned, his absence of little importance at the time to either Arthur or his mother. A few years later, despite always admonishing Arthur as a small child to obey the Highway Code, she herself stepped out into the road without looking both ways, an act of carelessness which allowed Arthur to inherit the family home.

Nearer to Arthur's heart however, were the changes at Aitcheson & Aitcheson. He became aware that things were no longer quite the way they used to be. Mr Aitcheson Senior retired along with Mr Wrigglesworth. Mr Aitcheson Junior took over the business – and several others to boot when the opportunity arose. He was 'ambitious' and 'forward thinking' with no time for 'nay-sayers' or 'dinosaur stick-in-the-muds'.

Soon there were fewer and fewer people in the building Arthur could recognise, and fewer and fewer people who could recognise him. Gladys and her tea trolley no longer patrolled the corridors. A drinks machine was installed on the landing at the top of the stairs. Bright young men in sharp suits and severe young women with padded shoulders gathered there holding coffee in paper cups and talking loudly in a language Arthur found difficult to understand. It involved 'visions', 'outcomes' and 'targets', and when he excused himself to pass them, they would smile wanly in his direction but otherwise ignore him. It was deeply troubling.

His little rituals became increasingly important, the comforting *swish* of the double doors as he came and went essential to his sense of well-being. Every evening, his desk cleared of every last scrap of paper, he'd count his progress along the corridor, round the corner, down the stairs and across the atrium, say, "Goodnight", to William, and feel the thrill of anticipation at the approbation the double doors would shower on him as he passed. *Yessss*. They at least recognised him for what he was – a solid, reliable stalwart of the firm.

That evening, the last thing he remembered was William saying, "Night, Mr Hepplewhite," before one of the double doors swung open, striking him full in the face. There was a blinding flash of pain, and then darkness.

★ ★ ★

It was good to get back into the routine again, Arthur thought, alighting from the bus and beginning his regular habit of totting up the number of paces between there and the familiar granite steps leading up to the front entrance. It had been a long time.

Despite his deep sense of satisfaction at being back where he belonged however, there was also a considerable weight of anxiety about standing too close to the doors. When he reached the top step, he actually stopped for a moment, his hand briefly touching his face where he'd been struck, half-expecting them to terrorise him again.

The left-hand door was opened for him however, and the familiar voice of William Pevensey greeted him. "Morning, Mr Hepplewhite."

Arthur tipped his hat. "Good to be back, William," he said.

The man smiled, looking mildly embarrassed. "Actually, it's Albert, Mr Hepplewhite – not William."

Arthur was confused. "Oh – I'm sorry. I – I..."

"Not to worry, Mr Hepplewhite. Glad to see you looking so well."

Albert closed the door. There was no *swish* or *yessss* of approval as he did so. Nothing, except perhaps a faint *clunk*. Arthur stood in the atrium struck by a sense of it not being the way he remembered it, although he couldn't say precisely what was different. It just was. Smaller, perhaps. And then there was the matter of William, who was really Albert.

Distracted by this, he climbed the stairs, counting as he went: "...thirty-five, thirty-six." He'd reached the top landing. There were no more steps. Hadn't there been forty-eight? He was certain there'd always been forty-eight. He leaned against the bannister rail and looked down into the stairwell, wondering for a moment if he'd miscounted the last flight. Carefully, he counted them off a second time. "...thirty-six."

Bewildered, he turned right and set off down the

corridor. He turned the corner. "...forty-seven, forty-eight." He was standing outside his office door. The name-plate had been polished ready for his return. "Forty-eight," he repeated to himself. Surely it should have been fifty-six? Or was he muddling up the number of stairs with the paces from the landing to his office? He looked back along the length of polished floor. It seemed much shorter, and there were definitely only six mahogany doors leading off the corridor – not ten. He'd been warned a knock on the head might have lasting effects, but he'd not expected this.

He stumbled into his office, relieved to find that this at least was as he remembered it. Tidy. Uncluttered. A place for everything, and everything in its place.

A batch of paperwork sat in his in-tray. He took off his coat and hat and hung them up on the coat-stand along with his umbrella. He must concentrate. Get back into the swing of things. But he found it difficult. His mind kept wandering off, worrying about William who was Albert; about the number of stairs; the distance along the corridor, and the six doors. Time slipped away, and to his horror, when he checked his watch, it was gone five-thirty and there were still several outstanding matters still in his in-tray demanding his attention.

When he'd finally ticked off the last item, it was gone six o'clock. Flustered, he hurriedly donned his coat and hat, snatched up his umbrella and half-ran down the corridor. He forgot to count the stairs as he hurried down them. In the atrium, William – or Albert – was nowhere to be seen, but the left-hand door had been jammed open, so he went scurrying out into the night air with the dreadful knowledge that he'd not only broken the habit of using only the right-hand door, but he'd missed his usual bus home.

That night, beset by troubling dreams, he over-slept.

The next morning, already in a harassed state, he got into a muddle with the buttons on his coat and missed his regular bus. When the next one arrived, an over-sized woman was sitting in his preferred seat three rows from the front. Feeling deeply aggrieved, he sat behind her fretting over his lateness and her unwelcome presence.

It was almost nine-thirty when he reached the august premises of Aitcheson & Aitcheson. As he climbed the steps, he realised to his horror he'd left his umbrella on the bus.

He rechecked the time on his watch as if this might turn back the clock. How could he explain himself? It was unforgivable. With his mind engrossed in the task of rehearsing his speech apologising for his lateness, he reached out and had to pull himself up sharp. The half-glazed mahogany double doors had gone. In their place was an immaculately shiny revolving door of gleaming glass. Mr Pevensey was standing on the other side, beckoning him in encouragingly. Thrown into confusion, Arthur stepped forward and found himself propelled forward at an alarming rate to be deposited in front of the doorkeeper with what could only be described as undue haste. "The door," Arthur said, pointing at the revolving monster behind him. "How... how long has it been there?"

Mr Pevensey frowned, then smiled indulgently at him. "It's always been there, Mr Hepplewhite. You know that."

Trying to cover his tracks, Arthur ventured to say of course it had, it just seemed a little over-enthusiastic this morning, and Mr Pevensey had just smiled and nodded.

Composing himself as best he could, Arthur mounted the stairs and pretended nothing was amiss. After only two flights and twenty-four steps, he found himself on the top landing. No – he couldn't be. That was impossible. But a quick glance over the bannister into the stairwell confirmed that's all there were – two flights. He turned quickly and stumbled down the corridor and round the corner towards his office. He reached it within a mere couple of dozen paces, acutely aware he'd only passed four doors on the way.

Flinging open his office door and finding everything as it should be, he collapsed onto his chair, his heart racing.

The paperwork in the in-tray seemed to be more than usual.

He was being irrational, he told himself. It was what happened when you'd had a nasty blow to the head, hadn't had a good night's sleep, missed your regular bus, lost your umbrella and arrived late. He must put all these little irritations behind him. He must concentrate.

Time ticked by. The amount of paperwork in the in-tray didn't seem to have reduced one jot. He really must concentrate. But it was difficult. He could just about persuade himself not to think too much about the evident shortcomings of his memory, but he couldn't quite dislodge the notion that the matter of the disappearing double doors was something else – something very different. He'd have to mention it to William – no – Albert that evening.

It was almost six-thirty by the time he'd cleared his desk. He felt utterly drained. He collected his hat and coat and closed the door behind him. Out in the corridor, only half the lights were on, the far end lost in Stygian gloom of impenetrable darkness. Perhaps the cleaners were trying to save electricity. He'd find the switch on the landing for the lights on the stairs and turn them off again at the bottom.

He set off, counting as he went. Fifteen. He stopped. Instead of the corner, he'd come face to face with a brick wall. His heart flew into his mouth. He turned and hurriedly retraced his steps, aware the lights were going out behind him and there were no doors either to his left or right. He half-ran past his office and into that part of the corridor on the far side of the building he'd never set foot in all the time he'd been there.

With sweat pouring down his face, he reached the landing, his delight at finding it still there, and fully lit, overwhelming him for a moment. He tore down the stairs, aware he'd only counted up to twelve before he was standing alone in the empty atrium. He glanced over his shoulder. No, he wasn't imagining it. The walls were beginning to close in on him from every side.

He could hear himself cry out as he threw himself against the glass panel of the revolving door, sending the whole structure spinning madly around with himself caught inside it like a whirling dervish. It wouldn't stop.

A moment later, there was a terrible bang. The door shuddered to a sudden and unexpected halt, throwing him out of the building into an untidy heap on the smooth granite slabs at the top of the steps.

Winded, he lay there for several minutes, fighting for breath, trying to make sense of what had happened. A panic attack? His imagination playing tricks on him? No, it could never be that.

He pulled himself together and struggled to his feet. Nothing broken at least, but he needed to sit down, talk things over with William – or Albert – and recover himself. He needed to concentrate.

But first there was the small matter of the door.

He braced himself and turned to face it.

The mahogany double doors stared back at him blankly, the bright light from the atrium spilling out through the half-glazing onto the granite slabs outside.

Listening to his heart thundering in his head, Arthur put out a tentative hand and pushed against the gleaming brass plate of the right-hand door. It didn't move. He pushed harder. It still didn't move. He pushed the left-hand door and that didn't move either. Determined not to be beaten, he braced himself against both doors and shoved as hard as he could. The doors remained rock solid: firmly shut; unyielding.

His vision blurring with mounting indignation, Arthur hammered his fists against the door. Surely someone would hear him. He hammered again and could only just make out some sign of activity within. His vision cleared a little. William – or Albert, his face a mask of horror, was standing transfixed looking down at a prostrate form sprawled out on its back staring up at the ceiling with vacant eyes, a stream of blood from a gash on the forehead running down across the face onto the parquet flooring.

"Oh my God, Mr Hepplewhite – are you all right?" Arthur heard him ask.

Arthur banged on the door again, louder this time, shouting through the glass. "I'm here, Albert! Outside!"

But Mr Pevensey didn't hear him.

UP ON THE ROOF

It's August. Hot. There's not been rain for weeks and I'm up on the roof keeping an eye on things as usual. There's this one spot that gives me a great view out to the south. It's slap bang between the shingles on the Ridley place and the peeling white boarding on the Skeltons' opposite. I can see way over the top of Morgan's fuel stop, all the way down Main Street, past Parker's Hardware, and clear beyond the edge of town to the Double D boundary fence and Coyote Ridge. That's where they come from. When they come. The clouds.

Okay, I'll admit it – they kind of scare me.

I didn't always feel that way. When I was a kid – you know, four maybe five years old – Pa used to take me up onto Coyote Ridge and we'd sit on Redback Rock and watch them grow.

They'd start off real small and fluffy. Like bunches of cotton seed. Then the sky'd haze over and they'd spread out, getting thicker and thicker and turn purple-black. Mean looking. They'd block out the sun and it'd go real dark. Like it was night. Then the wind would drop. You hardly dared breathe in case you cracked the sky wide open.

We'd just sit there – waiting.

The lightning would start somewhere back in the hills. It'd light up the sky behind Tall Man's Bluff and keep it up for hours before you'd hear the thunder. That's when Pa would bring me home and we'd be back safe on the porch before it got real close. We'd sit out there, Pa and me, on the rocker, watching the lightning. Hearing it crackle. Counting the seconds between a flash and the thunder rattling the windows. Then the rain would come down in sheets.

Those were the good times.

I was eight, I guess. Almost twenty years back now, but I remember that day like it was yesterday.

Yeah – it was another hot August afternoon and I was playing out back in the yard with my kid sister, Hayley.

Pa called out from the back door. "Hey, Tyler! There's growler clouds gatherin' over Coyote Ridge. Wanna come?"

"Sure," I said. I didn't want to play with Hayley anyway.

He was in a hurry that afternoon. I had to run to keep up with him. The clouds had gotten much bigger, he said. I guess he knew we'd left it too late. By the time we'd reached Redback Rock, there was blue and white forked lightning fizzing all round us. Pa was laughing. It was like the Fourth of July in town, he said, only bigger. I don't know why we didn't turn back. But we didn't.

Next day they came looking for us. Sheriff Vincent. Mr Hickson. The Parker brothers. The Ridleys and Skeltons. Ma had called up Reverend Brown and told him we'd gone up onto Coyote Ridge and hadn't come back.

When they got us down, they said it was the worst storm there'd been in years.

They said other things too. About how Pa must've been crazy taking me up there. About how God must've been smiling on me else I'd have surely been killed – like Pa. It must've have been a thunder bolt, they said. I don't know. I only remember it was the first time I saw it – the fiery ball of light coming out of nowhere. Hovering in front of us. Then the sound that made my ears hurt. And Pa being thrown in the air, landing on Redback Rock like a sack of potatoes falling off the pickup.

When they asked me what'd happened, I didn't tell them about Pa. About him laughing. About the red glow round Redback Rock afterwards.

I didn't tell them about the voices either. Not then.

I tried to forget about them. But they'd told me things. Secret things. They'd said Pa never understood. But I was different.

I guess I'd no idea what they meant being so young. But after that, every time a storm brewed up over Coyote Ridge, I could feel it coming. The hairs on the back of my head would stand up. That's when I'd hear them calling me.

Most times I couldn't go up to the rock. Ma used to keep me in my room when a storm was coming.

It was a couple of years after Pa died that Ma took sick. She got tired real easy and had to go to bed most afternoons. In the summer, me and Hayley pretty much looked after ourselves once school was out.

That's when I started going back up again onto Coyote Ridge.

This one day Hayley was out playing in the Skelton's back yard with her friend Ann-Marie. Ma was asleep and I got this feeling – you know – that a storm was coming.

I didn't tell Ma I was going up to Redback Rock. She wouldn't have let me go. But I could hear them calling, so I went.

I just sat there, waiting. Like Pa and me had done. Watching the sky go dark and everything go real still. And then it started – like always – the lightning lighting up the whole sky behind Tall Man's Bluff and the thunder starting to rumble somewhere a way off. I guess I must've been scared. I could feel the thunder coming up through the soles of my shoes, so I put my hands over my ears and closed my eyes. When I opened them the lightning ball was right there in front of me again. Maybe a couple of paces distant – no more. I could hear the air crackling and fizzing all around me.

I don't know what happened after that. Everything went black. I was out cold for a long time.

Ma never got over it, Hayley said.

Doctor Gotlieb at Bethlem Clinic has a name for it – when you hear voices in your head. I must've been telling him about them. I don't remember. He used electric shocks to get rid of them. Called it 'therapy'. I tried telling him I didn't want rid of them – that they told me things. But when it came to explaining, I wasn't good at it. I'd get my words all jumbled up and there'd be more therapy. So I reckoned it was better not to mention them again.

I met old Yellow Wolf at Bethlem. A Lakota Sioux. Born way back. He couldn't see no more but he heard real good. I told him about the voices. He understood. He said back in the old days, the young men would go up to Redback Rock and wait there, maybe three – four days without food. They'd sit up there just staring at the sun waiting for a sign. Course all that stopped when they got moved out onto the reservation up at Bad Water Creek. But old Yellow Wolf said when it was his time, he'd snuck off and come back to Redback Rock to see his sign. Said he'd sat up there three days when this great storm came in from the south. The sky'd gone blacker than a raven's wing, he said, and a fiery ball of light had come down out of the thundercloud and hung right there in front of him. Like the sun had dropped from the sky. He said he'd stayed real still, and voices had spoken to him in a strange tongue he could understand. Told him things. Sacred things. Told him he was a Chosen One and if he came back to the rock he could join the others. Said he'd promised he would. And then a great thunder clap had knocked him to the ground.

The sheriff and his deputies had found him next day. Couldn't get any sense out of him. Called him a crazy Injun and locked him up in the town jail 'til Doctor Gotlieb got him a place in Bethlem.

They'd never let him out after that, cos he kept on telling them about the voices.

I played dumb and so they let me come home.

Only I couldn't stop thinking about Yellow Wolf, and him not being able to get back up to Redback Rock. So come the next storm I went right back up there myself and told them why old Yellow Wolf hadn't come back like he'd promised.

I ended up back at the Clinic. Doctor Gotlieb said I needed more 'therapy'. I didn't like it, cos it got me all muddled afterwards, and my head ached. But at least I got to see old Yellow Wolf and tell him what I'd done, so he died happy.

I was in the Clinic a couple of months. Had more therapy. I couldn't handle school any more after that. Mr Baker said maybe it was best if I stayed home and helped out where I could. I guess he was right. I've done okay. Reverend Brown lets me mow his lawn now he can't manage things so well. And Mrs Henderson has me round to do her patch of grass at the front.

But once I was back home, I still heard them – the voices – when the storms came. Sometimes, if Ma'd given me my medication, I'd sleep through. But not always. The night she died I was up on Coyote Ridge. Sheriff Vincent took me back to the Clinic. I was there a good while – 'til they decided what to do with me.

Hayley married Billy Carter not long back. He's moved in with us. He's a good man. Understands voices in the head. Says there's no point in medication and therapy. Says love and just keeping watch is all that's needed. I guess he knows more than most. His sister Dolly heard voices. One day she walked out through their front door and never came back. Folks got up a search party, but they never found her. That's why Billy's promised Hayley he'd keep an eye on me. Says he'll make sure I don't wander off. I suppose I should be grateful for that. I don't like the Clinic.

He saw me coming up onto the roof just now, so I reckon he knows I'm watching out for clouds. I know they're coming, cos the hair's standing up on the back of my head.

Maybe it's not the clouds that scare me. Or the voices. Maybe it's the therapy.

I WANT TO BE THE ANGEL

Data-Slice 12: 03.12.2092

When these data blocks get accessed in 2192, most of this stuff's going to sound pretty weird. It's a record – that's all. About life up here. Dominic says, "Keep it short."

I'm Maximillian Hardinger. I was ten on 15th July. I got selected from the Year Six students to do the last data-slice on this block before it gets stowed away in the Academy Archives for posterity.

It's December – time for the UN Festival of Light again. Last year we celebrated Hanukkah with lots of candles. This year it's going to be Christmas. We're doing a nativity play and I want to be the angel. It's my last chance because I'll be a Foundationer this time next year. Foundationers go Earthside to study at one of the UN RECs – Regional Education Centres – they're the best.

Two of our tutors, Justine and Dominic, are organising everything as usual. Justine's a Christian Theist, so the nativity play means a lot to her. Dominic's a Total Atheist, but he still enjoys fixing the festivals. He's good at link-ups.

He has to be. We're based on different Orbiter Stations – all six of them – so the images have to be synched through the multi-track transjector network to achieve absolute visual unity on screen. One nanometre out and you can see the seaming.

Anyway, as I was saying, this year it's going to be Christmas. I'm provisionally tagged as a Magus – but I really want to be the angel.

The trouble is Gabriel's been tagged for that part already, which just about hangs my chances. He's on Orbiter 1 like me – same year too. He's also a Christian Theist with big ideas about himself. Says with a name like his he's a natural for the part. "Whoever heard of an Archangel called Max?" he says.

I just ignore him. (I'm going to be a Committed Humanist like Erik – my Dad. He says some people can't help being ignorant. Gabby's one of them.) At least I got one over on him during the auditions. I was the only guy who didn't smash into the scenery over-revving the mini-drive hover. I know that earned me plus-points as far as Dominic was concerned.

"Angels are supposed to 'appear'," Dominic says. "They don't *hyperdive*." Gabby hyperdives. Justine says she sure he'll improve with practice, but I doubt it. He's got finger-jerk reaction from playing too many quick-fire visi-boards. I'm going into bio-technology, so I never mess with them. You can't afford to if you're taking on something that needs ultra-sensitive manual control. (Dominic's put together a really difficult laser project for me to help sharpen up my concentration levels. It's nearly finished and Erik says he'll play it on the free-wall back home when it's ready.)

Iqbal – he's in Year Five on Orbiter 4 – says I should be hyper-glad about being a Magus because the costume's galactically spectacular. He's only tagged to be the Inn Keeper, so I guess he has a point. It's just that I really wanted to be the angel.

Erik says he doesn't care what I am as long as I act the part properly and put some feeling into it. During recreation last night we did a bit of research into the Data Store over the vidlink and came up with some background stuff.

Melchior means "King of Light". Erik thinks the part might be a good choice after all – especially with my laser project. I bring gold as my gift. It used to be special to royalty way back, but of course we all wear it nowadays. There's a processing plant on Moonbase churning it out.

Two other guys in Year Six have been tagged definite parts already. Elton's on Orbiter 2. He's going to be Joseph. He's welcome to it. Type-casting, I call it. He can be pretty much of a nerk sometimes – just the sort of guy to be fooled into taking on something he never bargained for. Teo's playing Balthazar from Orbiter 3. He's really got presence. Knows what he's doing. Got style.

After the play, we all meet up on Moonbase – all fifty of us – for the usual Moon-Meet Celebration for Orbiter students – and the Great Feast, of course. Moonbase Catering really know how to lay on a party. There's masses of fresh fruit and vegetables from the biosphere. (After Orbiter rehydrated menu-packs for a year, I can tell you that's really something.) Elton wants corn-on-the-cob. I'm bidding for carrots, and Teo wants baked stuffed apples. He keeps going on about them.

Justine says the Conference Centre's going to be decked out with a huge multi-glitter fountain with a hologram star on top, and masses of holly and mistletoe. (It's not real, of course. We can't have the real stuff because of the Infestation Regs. Something nasty like a plant virus or an insect colony transshipped from Earthside could wreck the Moonbase ecology, Dominic says.)

There's music and singing, and Santa arrives in the Shuttle with presents for the younger ones. Of course, I've grown out of all that stuff now. I know it's Hugo Wallace. He's Moonbase Controller. There's no harm in pretending though. It's great to see the little ones' eyes pop wide open when he comes huffing and puffing through the air-lock with his huge sack.

I might feel a bit sad this year when its all over. It's the last chance I'll get to meet everyone again before going Earthside. I get screwed up inside when I think about it – even now.

Today I asked Justine if there was any chance of me getting the part of the angel in the Foundationers' Resurrection Festival sometime. She laughed. Said there were too many opportunities already for Orbiter personnel to become angels – usually by accident.

I got to thinking after that – maybe being a Magus wasn't such a bad idea after all.

A WIMMERAH FOR MARY

"What's the matter, cret-head?" Otis spat copiously into the soft green undergrowth, just missing the outer margins of the terrain plotter spread out on the darkening ground in front of him. "Got jelly-guts already?"

Colby took another swig at his honk flask and returned it to his hip pocket. The rest of the squad looked on: silent; waiting.

Otis squinted up at Colby from his hunkered-down position, his thin lips curling into a sneer. "Just lay off that junk, squaddie. This is a Corellian Ranger Unit, not a honk-house party."

Colby grunted and fixed Otis with a blood-shot stare before turning his attention to the scrawny figure in pelts and fur cap squatting opposite. "Hear that, Klickman?" he asked casually. "Maybe you'd better not let on you're chewing blatweed. It could get you penalty points."

Klickman stopped chewing and gulped. His small ferret eyes darted between the two men.

Otis moved fast; faster than Colby could have expected so much bulk to shift in what seemed like a fraction of a second. A jarring punch with the kick of a jack-blaster caught him squarely in the belly. He gagged under the blow, sagging to his knees and clutching at his scrambled innards.

Otis shoved him onto his back with a jab of his boot. "Watch your tongue, cret-head. Scouts do what they goddam please." He gave Klickman a sideways glance. "So long as they do their goddam job," he added.

Klickman looked suitably relieved and grinned crookedly at Colby's prostrate form.

Otis casually sauntered back to the rest of the squad as though nothing had happened and hunkered down again, smiling broadly with large, uneven teeth at the new recruit who sat next to him. "Discipline, boy, that's what's needed," he said softly to the pale-faced youngster. "I didn't get these stripes without doing what I was told." He jabbed at the gold bands below the flying eagle crest on the sleeve of his dull grey metallic uniform. "You do what you're told, boy, and you'll go far. You see." And he winked knowingly.

"Yes, sir," Jigs said, glancing nervously past Otis to where Colby was dragging his large frame back into an upright position with considerable difficulty.

Otis jerked a thumb over his shoulder at the dishevelled figure as it shambled back towards them. "You take it from me, boy," he said, loud enough for Colby to hear, "that cret-head is going to be trouble." He raised his voice louder. "You heard why I got him?" Jigs shook his head. "To put some guts back into him, that's why. Left his own somewhere back in the Medallion Mountains along with the rest of his Unit. Shit his pants cos a bunch of shigging Brims caught them napping." He laughed maliciously. "Ain't that so, *ex*-Sergeant Colby?" And he laughed again.

Colby joined the others and squatted down next to Jigs, ignoring Otis and glaring balefully across the terrain plotter at Klickman's unshaven, evil-smelling presence with ill-concealed contempt. The rest of the squad, grey and silent like Medusa's victims, watched and waited.

Klickman grinned back at Colby and with grubby fingers unwound from its sta-kleen wrapper a small block of compressed pink blatweed. Still grinning at Colby, he cut off a chunk with his skinny knife and with exaggerated slowness began chewing on it methodically. The remainder he rewrapped carefully, stowing it for safety in the Brimmercanti fur pouch slung across his shoulder.

Colby grimaced and looked away.

Otis returned to the matter in hand, jabbing a stubby finger at the terrain plotter. "Okay, tomorrow I want Beta Squad to take out the lodges by the river here. Ex-Sergeant Colby – with me watching his every move – and Alpha Squad will hold back until the river route's cut off and then take out the three lodges at the edge of the clearing there." He indicated the two locations on the plotter and scanned the faces of the men squatting round him. "Any questions?" he asked, eyeing Colby, challenging him.

But it was Jigs who piped up. "Sergeant Otis, sir, what's the likely opposition?"

Otis's eyes narrowed. "They're Brimmercantes, boy. Expect anything. They've bucked the Corellian League. They've been warned. Now it's time to teach them a lesson.

That's all you need to think about when you go in there blasting."

Jigs looked unsure. He glanced at Colby and back to Otis. "Yes, sir."

Otis reached across and clapped a paw-like hand on the boy's shoulder. "Tomorrow night, boy, you'll be proud to say you were one of General Brinkmaster's Rangers – and you'll have that wimmerah you wanted."

Colby snorted, risking having his left ear torn off. But Otis was feeling benevolent enough by then to ignore him.

"Okay, no more questions?" Silence. Otis looked up at the darkening sky. Already the suns had set and the forest around them was becoming an amphitheatre of strange silhouettes. "Okay, squad dismiss. Colby, hand over that flask – and take first watch. Jigs – take the second."

The squad split up into twos and threes, hunting out their sleeping packs from the heap where they'd been dumped by the Ranger Unit Personnel Transporter. Otis blocked Colby's way, hands on hips. "The flask, squaddie. We don't want you spacing-out when you're on duty, do we?"

Colby handed over the flask, watching with red-eyed animosity as the sergeant downed the contents in three gulps.

Wiping his mouth with the back of his hand and belching loudly, Otis shoved the empty flask back into Colby's ribs. "Don't let me catch you with that stuff again, squaddie – d'you hear?".

Colby stowed the empty flask back in his hip pocket and said nothing.

The stars were up when Jigs silently eased himself out of his pack and left Otis and Klickman snoring loud enough to waken the whole of Cantos. He tip-toed across the sleeping bodies of the rest of the squad and found Colby sitting with his back against a smooth-barked scurra tree staring out into the fathomless blackness of the forest.

"Colby, it's me – Jigs," he whispered. "It's second watch."

Colby didn't look at him. "I'm not tired, boy. You may as well go back and get some sleep. You're going to need it."

"You know I can't do that. Sergeant's orders."

"Crap," muttered Colby.

"It's still orders," Jigs insisted.

Colby turned from his preoccupation of staring into blackness. He studied the boy in the half-light of the twin moons that had not yet risen fully over the wall of forest. "What the hell are you doing here, boy?" he demanded suddenly, his voice harsh and menacing.

Jigs looked confused.

"I mean what the hell are you doing here – here in one of Brinkmaster's Ranger Units?"

"Cos I believe in the solidarity of the Corellian League – like the rest of us."

Colby laughed, a low almost inaudible sound that hardly passed for laughter. "You really believe that crap?"

Jigs glared across the small space between them. "It's not crap!" he hissed back, angry at the big man's heresy. "If we're going to advance civilization in the Western Spiral Arm there's got to be solidarity. What's wrong with that?"

Colby shook his head sadly.

"Don't you believe in what we're fighting for? What's the point of being a Corellian Ranger if you don't?"

Colby pulled the boy closer by his uniform epaulettes, checking beyond him that Otis and Klickman were still asleep. "Look, boy," he hissed, "Ten years ago I joined the Rangers for the same reason you did – to advance civilization – not to advance some tin-pot general's political ambitions."

Jigs looked frightened. He didn't answer. The twin moons of Cantos finally rose over the forest mantle and reflected eerily in the whites of Colby's eyes.

Colby let him go, cursing. "You're a damned fool," he said, addressing no one in particular.

Jigs leaned his back against the scurra tree for support, squinting through the eerie moonlight at the heretic. "Are you saying the Brimmercantes aren't acting in defiance of the Corellian League?" His voice was barely a whisper.

Colby didn't reply.

"Well, are you? They massacred your Unit in the Medallions, didn't they?"

Colby's head snapped round, his eyes slits of anger. "You shouldn't believe everything you hear, boy. It was a bunch of *Idecantes*." He stressed the word. "Young bucks just out for jolts," he added, musing over the memory.

"But Brinkmaster told Congress –"

"I don't give a honk what Brinkmaster told Congress – they were Idecantes."

"But why would he say they were Brimmercantes if they weren't?"

Colby snorted. "You really don't know very much, do you, boy?"

There was silence between them for a moment. One of the night creatures of the forest called to its mate, an eerie, musical sound that echoed and re-echoed around the hills. Warm lush smells of scented wood bark wafted up the hill and a light breeze stirred and rustled the dry grasses wistfully.

Colby shifted his position slightly and turned to study Jigs more closely. The smooth face and spruce uniform made a stark contrast to his own dirty and over-worn appearance. "Look, boy," he said more gently, "I don't mean to turn your world on its head, it's just that tomorrow shouldn't be happening."

"The Brimmercantes have to be taught a lesson," Jigs insisted, repeating Brinkmaster's campaign slogan as though the previous conversation had never taken place. "They have to learn discipline."

"And they learn that by being blasted out of creation, do they?"

"We have to show them we mean business – as a warning to the others."

"Look boy, that's a village community down there," Colby said, pointing down into the valley bathed in the moonlight, "not a pack of howling yelkies."

"But the Brimmercantes aren't *human*, Colby," Jigs argued, and as if to prove it to himself he quoted Brinkmaster's favourite maxim. "They're a primitive alien life form."

Colby shook his head and began addressing the soft ground just in front of his boots, emphasising his words with expansive gestures. "Okay – so they're got honey-coloured fur and black-skinned tails – and maybe they don't look much like – or behave much like human beings. And okay – so they're hermaphrodite and we haven't a clue how they shig, but they've got a complete language and culture – they're not *animals*."

Jigs backed off. "All right, I won't argue the point, but they have to accept the New Order – they can't go on existing in an archaic tribal environment – not now."

"Who says so?"

"Congress, Colby." Jigs was getting exasperated by the big man's ignorance. "Cantos has to get back into line with the rest of the Annexed Worlds."

Colby shook his head again in disbelief. "Boy, this might just come as something of a shock to you, but the majority of the inhabitants on this little planet have never even heard of the Corellian League. Cantos was annexed sometime last century in name only. A few traders came back with a ship-load of artefacts and started shooting their mouths off about it being tribute – and jingo," he snapped his fingers, "the Corellian League decided Cantos was one of the Annexed Worlds!"

Jigs ignored this. "Well, anyway," he insisted, "it's for the greater good."

"You sound like Brinkmaster."

"And what if I do? I'm proud of it. He's a man of vision – a man for our times."

"Crap," muttered Colby again and turned to watch the river below as it became a silver ribbon of light through the ebony darkness of the surrounding terrain.

For a moment neither spoke. Then Jigs cleared his throat slightly. "What's the difference between an Idecanti and a Brimmercanti anyway?" he asked cautiously. "I thought Canti sub-groups were all the same – just had different customs?"

"Well you thought wrong."

"Don't they look the same?"

"Sure, exactly the same – like you and me look the same."

Jigs didn't know what to say. He looked away from Colby's black, thick-set scowling features and grizzled hair, and studied his own slim pale fingers as if seeing them for the first time in his life.

"They're the same *species*, dummy," Colby growled. "That doesn't mean they have the same coloured skins – or customs for that matter. The Brims blend with their forest. They're static communities with extended family lodges. They're a peace-loving, artistic – people." He chose the word deliberately.

"And the Idecantes?"

"Nomads. Hunters. They camp out in the open plains up north. They've got barred coats to camouflage them in the grassland. They live by their wits – their instincts – and they're a pretty terrifying bunch to meet up with."

"Then why did Brinkmaster blame the Brimmercantes for the Medallion massacre?"

"Simple. They're an easier target, aren't they? There's not much razz in trying to hunt down a band of Idecantes.

You never find them anyway. They find you. And when they do, you wish they hadn't." He remembered. "Brinkmaster wants to impress Congress with an expedition that gets results. If it looks good, Congress won't be asking questions. They don't give a shig how it's done, why it's done or if it means anything anyway. It *sounds* good, and that's all that matters. Brinkmaster knows that. And what's more, he knows there's a chance he'll get offered a preferred seat for services rendered."

"But they'll resist, won't they?"

Colby fixed Jigs with a red dead-eye gaze and shook his head slowly.

"You're lying!"

"No I'm not, boy. Down there," and he jabbed a finger towards the still silent valley, "is a group of unsuspecting, undefended lodges."

"Don't give me all that crap, Colby! How do they fend off the Idecantes?"

"You want to take back a wimmerah don't you?"

Jigs nodded. "Sure I do. I promised one to my kid sister. She saw one in the Galactic Artefacts Museum last year – said it was something she wanted more than anything else in the world."

"And you know what it is?" Colby asked ingenuously.

"A torque sort of thing they wear round their necks, that's all. So what's special about a piece of jewellery?"

"It isn't jewellery, boy, that's what's special about it. A wimmerah gives off ultra-high-frequency oscillations. Way back in the mists of time, when the Canti sub-groups split up, the Brimmercantes developed a low-frequency communication ability in addition to their language – all of it too low for the human ear. The Idecantes went the other way. They developed high-frequency levels as part of their hunting technique." He paused for effect, as though telling a fairy tale to a small child. "As soon as a Brimmercanti's born, it's given a family wimmerah. They're handed down generation after generation. Gifts from their gods, they say. Perhaps they were," he added, musing for a moment on the possibility. "Wimmerah are strange things, boy. On a Brimmercanti they're like externalised adrenaline. They react – especially to fear or panic. They vibrate. And when the oscillations reach a certain pitch Idecantes can't stand the noise – literally – it blows their minds."

Jigs was suspicious. "How do you know all this, Colby?"

Colby hesitated a moment before answering. "Cos I was sheltered by a community just like that one," he said softly, "before I made the return trip to Ranger Base after the massacre."

Jigs looked down into the valley and seemed to pale in the moonlight.

★ ★ ★

In the pre-dawn darkness, twelve grey-uniformed figures with jack-blasters and dome helmets strung across their shoulders, silently snaked their way down the flanks of the hill-side through a tangle of forest undergrowth. Five or six paces ahead of them, a gaunt figure swathed in Brimmercanti pelts ducked and bobbed, blazing a trail as he went.

In a small clearing, Klickman stopped and held up his hand. Otis brought the rest of the column to a halt. He squatted down and spread out the terrain plotter in front of him, motioning the rest of the Unit to gather round. He flicked on the back light, throwing the image into three-dimensional focus.

"We're here," he said, jabbing at the plotter. "From here on there'll be helmet communication only, is that understood? Otherwise, they'll pick up our voice tracks – and we don't want them all diving into the river, do we?" A vicious smile spread across his honk-flushed features.

Colby was hunkered down next to Jigs lost in thought, contemplating the depths of his dome helmet. Suddenly, he pulled at the boy's sleeve. Jigs ignored him, keeping his eyes firmly on Otis and the plotter. Colby tugged again. Jigs cast him a 'piss-off' glance and stood up, starting to fix his helmet in place like the rest of the Unit.

"Jigs!" hissed Colby, keeping his voice so low it was almost inaudible. "As soon as the action starts, get that helmet off fast. D'you hear?" Jigs opened his mouth to say something. "Don't argue – just do it!" His grip on Jigs' arm added an urgency to his insistence.

Jigs hesitated and then fastened on his helmet. His pinched, sleep-cheated eyes searched Colby's tense expression through the face-plate. He nodded, almost imperceptibly.

Colby slammed on his own helmet and began fastening the clasps.

"Okay," Otis's voice rasped through the intercom, "split

into attack squads. Klickman will lead Beta Squad to attack position Q. When I give the signal, clear out the river lodges as fast as you can. Alpha Squad will hold position Z to stop them making a break for the forest. As soon as the river lodges are cleared, Beta Squad's to hold the river approaches. Ten to one they'll bolt from the landward lodges once they realise what's happening. Alpha Squad can then finish them off with a pincer movement from the rear." He surveyed his Unit. "Okay, let's do it."

The party split up, Klickman bobbing and weaving ahead of Beta Squad as he led them off through the undergrowth until they were out of sight.

Otis swung round. "Colby! Up front. I want a cret-head where I can keep an eye on him."

Colby gave Jigs a parting glance and moved up the column to join Otis.

At the river, the clearing was bathed in thick blue shadows, the morning suns not yet high enough above the forest backdrop to cast their full light on the scene. The lodges were ranged around the clearing exactly as Klickman had reported, three set back against the edge of the forest and the remaining three spreading out from the river bank into the water.

From the outside the lodges weren't much to look at: domes of blue-coloured mud interwoven with branches and grasses that stood not much taller than an average man. Low doorways covered by some sort of multi-coloured material faced the river, and around them were strewn a variety of grass baskets and mud pots, and strange unidentifiable artefacts. They might have been implements or simply junk, it was hard to tell which.

A warm, musty smell lingered about the place and four or five small black and white striped creatures the size of dogs with squirrel faces, curled up contentedly against the outside of the lodge walls or grubbed around in the baskets for scraps.

The lodges themselves were perfectly silent, their occupants still wrapped in sleep.

Otis brought his squad to a halt at the fringes of the forest and fanned them out, two to a lodge. Colby he kept to himself. "I want to see you blow away a couple of these shigging Brims with my own eyes," he said quietly, jabbing Colby in the back. "I've been looking forward to watching you do it."

Colby looked impassively at the wolfish features behind the face-plate and said nothing.

They waited, Otis scanning the river bank for signs of the second party. After a while Klickman appeared briefly on a cleared path that ran alongside the river. Otis signalled to him and opened his long-range channel. "Okay Beta Squad, spread out."

Grey-helmeted figures, jack-blasters in hands, moved silently along the river bank, peeling off in twos at each lodge. The black and white creatures ignored the intrusion, too preoccupied with whatever they were doing. Klickman stayed on the fringes of the undergrowth, his part of the job already done.

Somewhere in the depths of the forest, a creature

whistled plaintively and then a hush settled over the place, expectantly.

"Now!" Otis's voice boomed down the communication's systems.

The figures by the river broke into action. With quick bobbing movements, they plunged through the doorways and almost immediately the firing began – or it could be assumed it began. The black and white creatures suddenly bolted for the forest and were gone.

Inside the grey helmets there was just the sound of laughing or swearing coming over the open channels. Only Klickman in his scout's cap could hear the sounds that really mattered: the thumping of the jack-blasters as they tore holes in whatever they were pointed at, and the screams of agony as they efficiently went about their business.

And then for Alpha squad, waiting for Otis to give them the go, it wasn't just audible any more – it was visual: a panorama of soundless confusion, panic and slaughter.

A young Brimmercanti made a mad dash from the landward door of its home. Colby watched it, its lithe young body turning and twisting to rush headlong for the river and comparative safety. Its eyes burned red with fear and its lips were drawn back against its sharp, white incisor teeth. Around its neck, the first shaft of morning sunlight struck the pale silver band of its wimmerah. In his brain, Colby began to feel a warning tingle, a hum that was beginning to sing. His hands flew up to his helmet catches.

"Jigs!" he screamed down the intercom. "Get it off!"

The boy was on the far side of the clearing. Colby saw

him wrench the helmet away as a long, agonising wail of pain ripped through the still morning air. There was the thump of a jack-blaster and the wail was cut off in mid-breath.

"Colby, you cret-head!" Otis was mouthing through his face plate. "What the shigging hell are you doing?"

The sounds of terror had disturbed the Brimmercantes inside the landward lodges. They tumbled out into the suddenly brilliant sunlight, confused and unready for what was waiting for them. Jack-blasters spurted into action, felling all that stood in their path: young, old, feeble and fit alike. The screams and moans of the injured and dying commingled, an obscene threnody.

Otis rammed his jack-blaster into Colby's back and shoved him forward. Colby twisted, knocking the blaster aside. Otis looked at him stupidly. The din from the dying swelled against the incessant drumbeat of death, reaching a crescendo of unearthly spine-chilling sound until the air seemed ready to splinter into myriad fragments. For a brief moment, Otis stood transfixed, his eyes bulging in their sockets and then his hands came up, clawing uselessly at his helmet. He reeled for a second and then crashed to the ground like a felled tree.

At the far side of the clearing, Jigs stood paralysed, staring at the scene unfolding before him.

Amidst the screaming and wailing, the thump-thump-thumping of the jack-blasters suddenly ceased. Everywhere grey figures were convulsing, contorting, clutching at their helmets, some writhing on the ground, others already strangely still. Rushing chaotically amongst them, terrified Brimmercantes were sprinting for the river and disappearing beneath the dark embracing waters.

Then there was nothing. Just a deathly silence over the place and ripples dispersing across the water. Scattered amongst the overturned baskets and broken pots was a random patchwork of bloodied remains, and sprinkled between them in frozen positions of pure agony lay the dull grey shapes of Brinkmaster's Rangers.

"Colby, what the hell happened?" Jig's voice was barely a whisper across the clearing.

Colby was watching the river bank, his eyes squinting against the slant of the morning sun. "I told you," he said dully, " – the wimmerah. When Brimmercantes panic, they vibrate. I reckoned the oscillations would get picked up and amplified by the communication channels." He glanced briefly at Jigs and then at the contorted bodies. "Looks like I was right."

Jigs stirred himself into action. He walked over to an untidy furry heap on the ground. A gaping crimson hole was spreading out across its back above the tail, the oblong head thrown back in the moment of agony, red eyes staring, teeth bared. The webbed fingers had clawed at the ground in their death throes. "No one said they would bleed," he said accusingly. "Not blood. Not red blood – like ours." He looked down at the unused jack-blaster in his hands and turned suddenly, throwing it as far as he could towards the dense blackness of the forest. Its fall was broken by a small leafy shrub at the edge of the clearing that quivered indignantly at the sudden assault.

"Nobody told you a lot of things, boy. Take a look inside the lodges. You might learn something."

Colby turned and left Jigs standing head bent amidst the carnage. Down in a patch of reeds by the river bank, something had caught his eye – the flash of a skinny knife.

"Klickman!" he bellowed, his big frame covering the ground between them. "Klickman! Stand up, or I'll blast you where you are."

The gaunt figure of the scout slowly emerged from the reed bed clutching the half-skinned body of a small Brimmercanti, its brains spilling out of its shattered skull like a half-eaten blueberry pie. Blood covered his hands, running in gaudy rivulets down his sleeves and staining his pelt leggings.

Colby stopped dead.

Klickman shrugged slightly and looked apologetic. "A man's got to make a living somehow," he said, a nervous smile twitching at a corner of his mouth.

Colby gagged, his stomach heaving involuntarily. He didn't wait to hear any more. Raising the barrel of the jack-blaster, he pressed the trigger. There was a dull thump and Klickman suddenly had a hole punched in his chest the size of a fist. At first there was nothing, as though Klickman's body had refused to believe what had happened, and then bright frothing blood began bubbling down the fringed jacket like a wet red curtain being lowered. Klickman sank to his knees, his dying eyes fixed on Colby with a look of total incomprehension. For a moment he didn't move; then slowly he crumpled up and collapsed into the dark waters, still grasping his grizzly trophy as the currents dragged him under and out of sight.

Colby watched the reddened ripples fade and then turned back to find Jigs. The boy was emerging from one of the low doorways, his fists clenching into tight knots and anger burning in his eyes.

"You've seen the dome paintings then?" Colby asked casually, knowing that he had. "They're really something, aren't they? Bet you won't see anything like them again in the whole of the Western Spiral Arm." He paused for effect. "Not bad for a primitive alien life form, eh boy?"

Jigs was too angry and confused to reply.

Colby left him to his anger and began stripping off his combat boots and uniform. He wrapped the lot into a tidy parcel and took it down to the river bank. With all his strength he hefted the heavy bundle out into the middle reaches and watched it sink rapidly beneath the swirling current. Then he turned back to clear the place of its garbage.

One by one he dragged the contorted bodies of the Rangers down to the river and shoved them in, letting them float away to some anonymous grave downstream. He moved Otis last, finding him difficult to shift. Eventually, the lifeless hulk slithered down the blue mud banking like a bloated bladder. For a while Colby stood watching, waiting for the river to take its grey cargo around the bend and out of sight.

Behind him, Jigs was still standing mute and immobile. Ignoring him, Colby collected the jack-blasters and stacked them neatly in a row against one of the lodges, even retrieving the boy's from where it had landed in the shrub at the rim of the forest.

Then he began the sickening task of collecting the Brimmercanti dead and bringing them to the centre of the clearing. He carried them all carefully, reverently, trying to arrange the tangled, bloodied limbs in the order he remembered Brimmercanti custom demanded. He closed glazed eyes and open mouths and gave them all a semblance of peace: it was the best he could do.

Where he could, he kept them in family groups. Where he couldn't, he placed them separately, so as not to offend. It took him a long time. In the end, the only bodies remaining were the two sprawled out untidily in front of the boy.

Jigs had finally moved and was standing over a dead Brimmercanti still clutching its young to its breast. The same shot had stamped a hole clean through them both, leaving a trail of shattered bone and tissue in its wake. From what was left of the lifeless little heap of bloodied fur still clinging to its parent, Jigs carefully unclasped the wimmerah. He straightened up slowly, turning and fingering the smooth unworked silver shape in his hands as if it were a fragile, living thing. It gleamed softly, responding to his touch.

Colby watched, hands on hips. "Well," he said gruffly, "you got your wimmerah. Your kid sister should be real pleased."

The boy looked up slowly. Colby was a terrifying figure, his strong black body smeared in blood and foul-smelling fluids. Jigs shuddered, trying to control the urge to gag. "Will they come back?" he asked, choking on his words.

"In a day or so."

Jigs looked over to where Colby's meticulous handiwork lay spread out in tidy lines, a grotesque monument. He bent down, replacing the wimmerah around the still-warm little neck, feeling the soft fur caressing his hand as he did so. He stayed there, hunkered down with his head bent, his hand resting on the shattered bodies for a moment.

Colby waited respectfully for a while. "There's work to be done here," he said at last. "I'm staying on." There was no immediate response. "You'd better go. There's your kid sister. It's only a two day trek back to the Transporter rendezvous. You can say you got separated from the Unit on the night march – got lost. Act like you've gone crazy for a while and you'll get your discharge easy enough."

Jigs turned from watching the blood trickling across the back of his hand. His pale eyes were clouded.

Colby went on. "We won't be the last Rangers out for easy pickings – Brinkmaster will see to that. But the next time they come –" he nodded in the direction of the jack-blasters, their ultra-photosensitive particle energisers constantly recharging "– it'll be different." He smiled grimly. "It's time the Brimmercantes had more than their fear to rely on."

Jigs straightened and stepped back, wiping his hand on the sleeve of his uniform and smearing the crest of the flying eagle with tracks of blood. He watched impassively as Colby bent down and picked up the last sad burden from in front of him, cradling the bodies in his strong, black arms and carrying them across to join the others. He followed, silently watching the big man finish his grim task.

When it was done, Colby straightened and turned, challenging the boy with a penetrating gaze. He hadn't long to wait. Their eyes met.

Pale with anger, Jigs nodded and began yanking off his combat boots.

APOLOGIA

URGENT REQUEST FOR REPATRIATION

I wish this to be known.

I meant no harm.

I do not put this forward to excuse My actions. They are inexcusable. I did not heed My Mentor's warning. I was not sufficiently prepared. My curiosity overcame My reason. This was wrong. I accept this. The fault is Mine and Mine alone.

I ask for Your forbearance.

The woman I know as Mother is crying. I have made Her cry again. I recognise this is not acceptable.

I cannot explain to Her the things I have done. Or the things I have said. They are logical to Me. But not to Her. And I cannot identify the appropriate response patterns She expects of Me.

I understand now I have the power to hurt. This was never My intention. I have never done this willingly or knowingly, but because I am what I am. I acknowledge I lack the wisdom to rectify this.

We are not compatible.

I acknowledge I have failed.

STATEMENT TO THE COUNCIL

From the beginning I understood there would be two Entities – a Man and a Woman. I comprehended this and Their separate and distinct biological functions which are replicated in many life-forms We have studied. But I could not comprehend the logic-base of Their reference terms. They have several identities. Derek and Sandra. Mr Webster and Mrs Webster. Father and Mother. Daddy and Mummy. I understood and continue to understand only the excellence of Unity and the independence of Individual Existence. Multiple identity is not compatible with this concept.

Other actions are contrary to Our understanding of Wholeness.

When I first arrived, the Mother tried to feed Me from Her biostructure. This distressed Me greatly. I was aware I was hungry, but could not accept Her sacrifice of Self. Unity is completeness. It must not be violated. Energy given to Another depletes the Life Source. Frequency of such action will lead to extinction. I could not communicate this fear. I could only turn My head away. This would make Her cry.

When I would not deplete Her Life Source, the Man gave Me warm nutritionally balanced fluids from a small bottle. Afterwards I would sleep. This was a new experience for Me which I found very pleasant until I needed to evacuate waste products. I understood from neuron-impulses that this process was essential to prevent the malfunction of My biostructure. Confined by My immature state however, I was not able to remove Myself from these waste products and found it necessary to attract attention. This was not easy. I had not understood that lexicon-based communication skills are not immediately available to the immature form of this Species. Only sounds.

When I made these sounds, the Woman would come. Sometimes when it was dark, Father would come. If I made these sounds too often, Father came less. Then only the Mother came. And when She came, She gave me a new concept of Time. She would say – "It's only two o'clock – three o'clock – five o'clock" – or – "This is the third – fourth – fifth Time tonight, Little One. Go to sleep. Mummy's tired."

But if I made sounds, she would still come. This was not logical.

As I grew, My speech units improved. I found I was able to communicate, but only with limited success. This was very frustrating for Me. If I wanted something, it was often much simpler to open My mouth and expel atmospheric intake under pressure to make the maximum noise possible.

Later, I also learned to stand on My legs – and to walk. This is a strange but satisfying experience I cannot explain to You. Once I could walk I discovered I could do more things.

As I grew, I learned to climb out of the place they put me in when the darkness came. I began to explore My surroundings. The Man and Woman had surroundings of their own. They called these Their Room. They went there to sleep when it went dark. I was not aware this Species required so much sleep. There were no references to the extent of this practice in My tutorials. I became curious. I would wake them up and ask why They needed it. I did not always understand the reply.

Like Me, They would also make strange noises in the dark. These were loud and indicated some distress. This would make Me anxious. I would go into Their Room to ensure Their safety. When They saw me, I sensed Great Anger. Father shouted at Me. He shouted at Me every time I did this.

Mother would take Me back to My Room. "Let Mummy and Daddy have more time to themselves, Little One," she would say.

I did not understand Her meaning.

Their Time is not My understanding of Time. It is strange. It has many meanings. The division between light and dark. The space between two sequential, but not essentially connected events. Of beginning and ending. Of the past, the present and the future. Of limiting limitlessness. It is impossible to understand.

Mother would say – "It's time for breakfast – lunch – tea – supper – to go to bed – to get up – to get dressed." She had no comprehension of the ineffable beauty of Eternity.

I discovered Their Time is governed by this thing They call the Clock. It is a circular object they fix to Their walls. They have smaller ones They put on Their arms. It has duodecimal digits distributed equally around the circumference. The meaning of these digits is mysterious and inexplicable. In the centre of the Clock is an axis with two pointers of different lengths that move round slowly at different speeds. This represents Their understanding of Time.

I began to study this concept. I learned it caused hurt and other non-explicable reactions.

When Father came home to Us, Mother would ask – "What time do you call this?" She would point at the Clock and they would shout at each other until He went out again. After He had gone, Mother would sit staring at the Clock, watching the pointers going round many times. I deduced It required Constant Vigilance and Absolute Obedience. This was not logical.

Father came home less and less. Then He no longer came at all. Mother cried and picked Me up. She made My face wet. This was not pleasant. When I struggled, She put Me down. Then She went to Her Room and stayed there. She would not let Me in when I went to see Her.

So I dismantled the Clock.

I stood on the chair in the kitchen and took the Clock off the wall. I analysed its Functions. It had a logic circuit but no logic. I decided it was meaningless and put it in the waste disposal unit under the sink. I thought not having the Clock would make Mother happy again.

She was not happy. She was angry. She struck Me several times on My legs. My skin stung. Then She held Me to her very tightly, and said She loved Me. This was not rational. My attempts to explain My actions were frustrated by My immature speech units.

I went to My Room to conceptualise. Here I could talk to the Lion.

The Lion was something I had been given when I was small. It was inanimate, yellow and furry and was known as Leo. I could find no immediate functional use for its presence. However, as I grew, I discovered I could channel a variety of interactive stimuli into its fabric without causing any damage. By inverting My response patterns and inserting them into the low-energy fields within its molecular structure, I could construct a logic-based counter-response pattern with which to establish a dialogue whenever I chose. I then had a Compatible Entity – a valuable resource interface with which I could communicate.

Using the Lion, I began to analyse the non-logic-based reaction stimuli around Me and compute the probability of multi-variable output reactions to precisely defined input stimuli – or non-stimuli. Random, inexplicable events did not always compute to My satisfaction.

To explain. I had fallen over. At this stage of My development, I did not always have complete control over My Co-ordination. Part of My leg struck the ground and important fluid leaked out. It was red and sticky.

Mother picked Me up and said – "Don't cry."

I did not cry. I have learned that this hurt disperses in direct proportion to the bioregenerative properties of the organic structure that is damaged. I understood the hurt would pass.

She treated the damage with a strong-smelling liquid and afterwards covered it with a protective patch. She said I was very brave and She would kiss the hurt away.

Kisses do not eradicate hurt. They are a non-functional

use of the feeding orifice. They are not relevant to the healing process. I said I did not want to be kissed. This made Her cry again. I did not understand I was causing hurt by saying this.

She said She loved Me.

This is another inexplicable concept.

I consulted the Lion again.

"What is this Thing called Love?" I asked. I lacked a compatible interface between comprehension and suitable lexicon reference points with which to establish an adequate understanding.

The Lion told me – "It is an indeterminate illogical response pattern existing between Entities. It is a state of mind not linked to reason. It is an unreliable concept. It has an imprecise nature and lacks identifiable parameters. It is Their Master. It demands the giving up of the Individual Will to Another. The subservience of Self. It is like the Clock."

I said I had destroyed the Clock. Was it a bad thing to destroy Love?

The Lion said that it was.

I did not want to destroy Love.

The Lion said it was possible to destroy it without intending to. It explained to Me that – "When Love is demanded of an Entity from several other Entities, the First Entity becomes conflicted. More Love given to one Entity diminishes the Love given to Another. This causes hurt to the rejected Entity. The hurt is real. It is not the same hurt caused by an abrasion to the exterior fabric. It is a different hurt. There is no visible damage to the external biomorphic structure. This hurt is therefore more difficult to heal. It lies within the range of non-logic-based reaction stimuli.

This gave Me cause to re-evaluate past events. "Did the Man feel this hurt when he went away?"

The Lion said that He had.

"But I did not ask the Woman to Love Me and not Him."

The Lion said this was not relevant.

I considered this new knowledge. It was not satisfactory. It did not match any reference point available to Me. It was therefore beyond My experience and ability to compute.

Today, by My Mother's concept of Time, I am Four. And Today, I have caused Her great hurt again. It is the measure of the non-compatibility between My logic responses and Her lack of them.

Today I was given what She called a Birthday Present – a Special Present made by Her. She said She gave it with Love and hoped I would like it. I recognised what it was. I have several similar coverings in soft grey fabric. They are what She calls Track Suits although they do not run on tracks or are in any way compatible with them. On one shoulder She had put a circular representation – a yellow sphere with red equatorial bands against a black background. But there were nine stars in this background. I was confused. I tried to explain. I said – "Mummy, from Thepsis there are only five visible-spectrum light sources to the nova-side of Enklipte – not nine. Why have You made nine?"

I did not understand why this caused Her hurt but I saw that it did. She looked at Me in a strange way I had not seen before and started shouting, "No! No! No!" I did not like this. It frightened Me. Then She turned from Me and ran to Her Room shutting the door very loudly. I could hear Her crying and calling on God to help Her.

What is God? This is another non-concept.

I put on the suit. It fitted me very well. So I went to My Room to consult the Lion.

The Lion said I had destroyed Love. Mother had become a rejected Entity. This upset Me.

I understand now I have caused too much hurt. I cannot rationalise the response pattern expected from Me. I am not able to give Love or receive It. I recognise it is not possible to continue the Project.

ACKNOWLEDGEMENT OF OUTCOMES

I accept My existence here must be terminated.

I understand this will involve inconvenience and difficult reconfiguration to loop back the Continuum of Eternity to the point of Absolute Exactness at which I first Became.

I understand that in the New Beginning, it will not be Me, but the True Entity belonging to the Mother and Father in My place. The True Child. And from that point in the Continuum all will be well. I am hopeful this will be so.

I apologise to My Mentor and accept the censure imposed on Me.

I understand I will be demoted to the rank of First Novitiate for My Hubris and will not be allowed to participate in future Projects without the consent of the Full Council.

I am contrite and will learn from past mistakes.
I am ready to receive further instruction and guidance.

★ ★ ★

I again wish this to be known.
I meant no harm.

CONTRABAND

"Hi, Marty. Hey – can you do me a favour?"

There was no response to this suggestion. Deakins could feel the negativity beaming down to him through the silence.

He tried again. "I know it didn't work out too well last time…"

Maybe that wasn't the best tack to take. The silence deepened.

"Okay – I'm in a spot of trouble," he said coming straight out with it. No point in beating around the bush any longer. Marty knew him too well.

"What shit have you got yourself into this time?"

"I brought back something from the Outer Rim."

"You brought back 'something' from the Outer Rim," Marty parroted back at him, his voice heavily laced with sarcasm.

"Yes."

"And now you want me to help you get it back?"

Deakins tried to pass this off with a light-hearted chuckle. "Kind of," he said, hearing Marty's contempt bellowing through the verbal vacuum that followed. "Actually, I think it wants to go back itself," he added, as if this explained everything.

"Would you like to expand on that, Nathan?"

It was difficult to know where to begin.

"Look – I'm being very, very patient here, Nathan, but if you don't start coming up with something I can make sense of, I'm not interested."

"Well – okay. It's a polymorph."

"A what?"

"A shape-shifter."

"They don't exist, Nathan. You know that."

"Well, actually they do," Deakins insisted, keeping his voice down. "I've got one – right here – with me – right now."

"Just what are you high on this time, Nathan? GKM?"

"You know I don't touch that stuff any more, Marty. It's lethal."

There was an audible snort of disbelief.

"No, honestly, Marty. I gave up on all that crap months back – after I nearly blew my brains out."

"Well, like I said, Nathan, shape-shifters don't exist."

"That's what they want you to think."

"Who are 'they', Nathan?"

"Security."

"And you just happened to overhear a couple of them talking this over, did you?"

"No. I got it from a guy I was with. He sort of let it slip out."

"How high was he at the time?"

"He wasn't. Well – he'd never admit to it."

"And what did he say?"

"That there were a whole bunch of these things near one of the Outer Rim colonies. Security slapped a clamp-down marker on everything as soon as they heard of them. They were shit-scared. No messaging – no communicating – and definitely no contact."

"And you got curious?"

"I'd heard rumours. You can't keep the wraps on something as big as that."

"Not in the company you keep."

"I've got contacts, Marty. I can't help that."

"And one of them just happened to say, 'Hey, Nathan, guess what? I've got some hot property you really can't live without – a bug-eyed monster that can shape-shift into another bug-eyed monster.' Is that about the size of it?"

"I'd rather it didn't hear you say that," Deakins said, trying to get across the importance of this. "It can get *really* upset."

"Okay, no disrespect to your little friend, Nathan."

"You'll help me out then?"

There was a long pause.

"Please, Marty. I don't know who else to ask." Deakins hoped he sounded desperate enough to be taken seriously.

"Next thing you'll be telling me you can you get it to shape-shift into something that won't scare the shit out of the engineers when they see it." Marty's sarcasm had all the liquid viscosity of treacle.

Deakins tried to sound positive. "Sure. I can manage that."

Marty seemed to be giving this some thought. "Okay," he said finally. "Bring it on down to Hanger Ten. I'll see what I can do. Just get it presentable, will you?"

"Sure thing. See you in a couple of hours then?"

"Yeah – right."

★ ★ ★

Marty Veigler was waiting for him outside the office to Hanger Ten, hands firmly planted on his hips, his bulky frame filling the doorway. Deakins could feel himself and his little friend coming under Marty's close scrutiny from a couple of hundred yards away.

"You made it then?" Marty called out across the taxi-way, studying the four-legged hairy object trotting obediently next to Deakins on a lead.

When they reached the office, Deakins stopped and his hairy friend squatted next to him, tail wagging, gazing up at him with intense devotion.

Marty didn't budge from the doorway. "It's a dog," he said, folding his arms and giving Deakins the benefit of a withering glance.

"No – it's not, Marty. It just looks like a dog."

"It's hairy, got four legs, two ears, two eyes, a tail and a wet nose, Nathan. It's a dog. It even smells like a dog – a wet dog." He wrinkled his nose in disgust.

Deakins shook his head. "It's *not* a dog, Marty," he insisted through clenched teeth, keeping his voice down. "It was the best I could come up with to get it here, that's all. You said you didn't want me to scare the shit out of the engineers..."

Just to prove the point, one of the maintenance crew came out from the hanger and sauntered past, waving to Marty as he went. "Nice dog you got there, Veigler."

"It's not mine," Marty said, scowling at the man's back.

"You see?" Deakins said, relieved his subterfuge had worked. "It was the best I could come up with."

Marty snorted and waved Deakins to follow him into the office. "You can bring the mutt in with you," he said dismissively, "as long as it minds its manners. Has it got a name – or what?"

"Hengist," Deakins said, following in Marty's wake, his friend trotting dutifully beside him.

"What sort of name's that for a dog?"

"It's not a dog," Deakins reminded him.

"Sorry. I forgot."

Marty shoved a hot, strong coffee from the office drinks machine in Deakin's direction and sat down behind his desk, indicating Deakins might like to occupy the spare chair on the other side.

Hengist laid his head on Deakin's knee and looked up adoringly into his eyes.

Marty watched the pair of them over the rim of his mug. "So where did you pick it up?" he asked.

"On Delta Four."

"What were *you* doing on Delta Four?"

"Trying to earn some credit. You know how it is with me."

"Yeah, I know how it is with you. You're bloody useless. What were you this time? Baggage handler fourth class?"

Deakins shrugged off the insult. He deserved it. "Not exactly."

"And how come 'Hengist' there got onto Delta Four without anyone noticing? Dogs aren't allowed on board."

"A guy from the mining colony brought him up."

"As what?" Marty asked, a broad grin spreading across his face betraying precisely what he thought of the story so far.

Deakins felt stupid. "As part of his hand baggage," he explained lamely.

"Well, he would, wouldn't he?" Marty observed with a sage nodding of his head, and an expression that said it all. He cast a quick glance in Hengist's direction, sizing him up. "A large piece of baggage, was it?" he asked.

"Not that large actually," Deakins assured him. "That's why it was easy to –"

"To what, Nathan?"

"To – pick it up."

"Pick it up?"

"Well – walk off with it. That was the deal. He'd get it onto Delta Four. I was in baggage handling. I'd pick it up, get it back down and..."

"And then what? You'd *sell* it?"

Hengist blinked and looked anxious.

"No – nothing like that," Deakins assured him. "I'd keep it. Look after it. Have it as a pet."

Marty put down his mug and shook his head. "You must think I was born yesterday, Nathan. When did you ever have a pet?"

"I had a white rat when I was nine," Deakins said

defensively, feeling distinctly peeved that Marty should think him incapable of looking after another creature. "Nearly broke my heart when it died."

Marty rolled his eyes. "Okay, so you get Hengist here back to Earth as a handy piece of baggage and then what? You kept him on top of the wardrobe?"

Deakins was indignant. "Of course not! Once it knew it was safe, it could relax – shift back into…" He struggled to find the right word. "Into itself," he finished lamely.

Marty leaned across the desk and smiled broadly at Hengist who seemed distinctly unhappy at being scrutinised so closely. "And just how does Hengist look," Marty asked, "when its being 'itself'?"

Deakins could feel sweat breaking out on his face. "You don't want to know," he said. "Honestly, Marty, you really don't?"

Marty raised a sceptical eyebrow.

"It's not – pretty," Deakins explained. "Bit of a shock, really. Not very nice. I mean – you really don't want to *see* it."

Marty leaned back in his chair and folded his arms. "Well – you just describe it to me then, Nathan," he said, fixing Deakins with an unflinching gaze.

Deakins gulped, hardly knowing where to begin. "Let's say, it's a bit messy – well, maybe very messy, if you know what I mean."

"Go on."

"Phew, Marty – you're not going to like this, but okay, if you really want to know."

Marty nodded.

"Well – it's about the size of..." Deakins scanned the office trying to find something to use as an example. "The drinks machine," he said, thinking this was about right. "And it looks like a segmented pink rubber balloon on a big sucker that's oozing greeny-coloured gunge – like a slug trail – only bigger."

Marty was still nodding, paying close attention.

Deakins gave Hengist a friendly scratch behind one ear, hoping it wouldn't take offence. "It's not got a head – well not one that you'd recognise anyway – a bit like an octopus, except it isn't. It's got four antennae things coming out of the top with red blobs on the end – and a biggish hole underneath with orange suckers round it. I guess that's its mouth. I mean, I've seen it stuffing things in there with its feelers – arms – whatever – and making sucking noises. It doesn't smell so good either. A bit like rotting fish."

Hengist looked round at Marty with a doleful expression and whined softly.

Marty sucked on his teeth thoughtfully. "And it's told you it's homesick," he said, giving Hengist the benefit of his smile.

"Not exactly," Deakins admitted. "I just can't look after it, that's all. I mean, it's not like a pet rat, is it?"

"Or a dog," Marty observed helpfully.

"Exactly."

"Just keep it as a dog, then."

"I would, if it was that simple."

"Well, what's the problem?"

"It can only eat when it's 'itself'. And then – Marty, you

145

wouldn't believe what it eats…" Deakins shook his head at the thought of it.

Marty was waiting to hear the worst.

Deakins took in a deep breath and ploughed on. "Well – you know – it eats anything that's 'gone off' a bit," he began, recognising this was something of an understatement.

"Like all the out-of-date stuff in your fridge, Nathan?"

"Not exactly…it sort of prefers the gunk in the garbage can – and then – and then it spews out what its system can't process. You get the idea?"

Marty nodded. "Not house-trained then?"

"You could say that."

Marty mulled over what was expected of him. "So how am I supposed to get it back to Delta Four, Nathan?"

"The same way it came here – as hand baggage – with me."

Marty wasn't exactly convinced. "And just how will you 'persuade' it to shape-shift back into a leather hold-all?"

"It responds to visual or tactile stimuli."

Hengist yawned and lifted a paw, seeking attention. Deakins resumed scratching it behind the ears.

"That could be fun," Marty observed drily.

"Well, yes it was – to begin with – showing it a load of 3D holograms of different animals and other things – letting it rummage around the place as a garden gnome – but it couldn't go on like that. I mean, I couldn't handle the slime."

"Or the spewing up."

"Exactly."

"Understandable."

Deakins waited, wondering what Marty would decide. He really had no idea what he'd do if Marty didn't help him out.

"Okay," Marty was saying. "I'm taking a freighter out to Delta Four the day after tomorrow. Eighteen-hundred. I'll get you signed up as a baggage handler. You make sure you get that thing sorted out before you get on board, okay?"

Deakins breathed a huge sigh of relief. Hengist looked hopeful and stood up, wagging his tail.

★ ★ ★

Marty waited until Deakins had gone through the perimeter fence with Hengist in tow before he activated the communications channel.

"Hi, Security – Marty Veigler here. Deakins has just left. Yeah – you were right. Wanted me to wangle him a return trip to Delta Four. Gave me a whole spiel you'd have to be a half-brain to believe. Wanted me to help him get a shape-shifter back home. Yeah, I know. Crazy. I've logged him in as a baggage handler on the eighteen-hundred the day after tomorrow. He'll be carrying an extra bag. Think you might find its contents interesting. Yeah. Contraband, like you said. Most likely GKM."

Marty shut down the connection, satisfied he'd done the right thing this time. No more being taken for a sucker by Nathan Deakins. No, sir. Not ever again.

He served himself another coffee and leaned back in his chair. There was definitely an odd smell he hadn't noticed before. He sniffed at the contents of his mug. No, the coffee was fine. He leaned forward across his desk, the smell getting stronger. Like rotten fish.

On the floor where the dog had been sitting, and from there to the office door, was a trail of thick green slime.

LIFE EXPECTANCY

Fischer couldn't believe his luck. "There!" he said triumphantly.

Medlyev sighed and shook his head sadly. "Fischer, my friend," he said. "You are definitely – how shall I say? – one planet short of a solar system?"

"Look!" Fischer insisted, stabbing his finger against the observation pane. "It's as clear as day!"

Medlyev sighed again and half-heartedly gave the gleaming flat desert space between the towering outcrops of glittering granite and quartz a cursory glance.

"See it? Curving away to the right into that canyon? A track! It's definitely a track!"

"Okay, it could be a track."

"How much more of a track does it have to be, before you believe me?"

Medlyev didn't answer. He turned his attention back to navigating the surveyor.

"At least go round one more time, Oleg," Fischer pleaded. "Just for me."

Medlyev looked pained. "You always do this to me, Fischer. Every time we come to Gammos it's the same."

"That's because you won't believe your own eyes."

"I know what I see. I see rocks in a desert."

"But they move, Oleg. They're never where we saw them the last time around."

"They move because the wind moves them," Medlyev said with a dismissive shrug.

"Aw come on, Oleg. The wind's never *that* strong on this side of Gammos."

Medlyev pulled a face. "Who knows what it takes?" he said. "A thin atmosphere – low gravity – and *puff.*" He blew away a non-existent feather from the palm of his hand to demonstrate how little effort would be needed. "There you have it. Your rocks move."

"If there was a wind strong enough to move those damned rocks, Oleg, there'd be no tracks left, would there?" Fischer objected, sensing a flaw in his friend's argument. "They'd be wiped out. Besides," he added for good measure, "it took more than wind to move those rocks down in Death Valley, didn't it?"

A wry smile spread across Medlyev's solid features. "Of course," he said offhandedly. "It was ice-melt moving them around on mud. Those crazy oceanographers proved it."

"There's not been ice on Gammos for millennia – you know that. So what's moving that rock?"

"Perhaps it was those Little Green Men," Medlyev suggested, laying on the sarcasm thick and heavy with a trowel. "Now, if you don't mind, can we please get on with what we're supposed to be doing?"

Fischer's exasperation got the better of him. "Aw come

on, Oleg – aren't you just a *bit* curious about what's going on here?"

"No."

"Why not?"

"Because I don't believe rocks move around under their own steam, as you would say."

"What is it with you? Why can't you get your head around the fact there might – just might – be different life forms out here?"

"Because it's not a fact, my friend – and because no one's ever found a single species that isn't carbon-based, that's why."

"That's only because everyone's closed their minds to the possibility, that's all."

Medlyev remained unconvinced. "Fischer, my friend, do you know what your trouble is? You're an unrepentant lithophiliac."

"And you're nothing but a pig-headed geocentric carbon chauvinist!"

"Okay. Okay. I confess it," Medlyev said, throwing up his hands in mock capitulation. "I'll sign the paper. I'll do anything."

"Anything?"

Sensing Fischer had taken advantage of his unguarded offer, Medlyev backed off. "Well – not quite anything."

"Go around again?" Fischer suggested.

"Huh – and after that? Then what? Perhaps we see some more tracks. Where does that leave us? You know I can't land the surveyor without permission. We're on a fly-past.

Looking for strata shifts. New seams to exploit. That's all they want. Who's going to give permission for a ground survey – chasing rocks across a desert on the say-so of a crazy intern? No one. Forget it."

"I could go down with a pod," Fischer suggested, trying not to sound too pushy.

"Hah! Now I know you're definitely crazy!"

"I've done it before."

Medlyev raised one very bushy eyebrow in disbelief. "When?" he wanted to know.

"A couple of years back – with Zhukhov."

Medlyev paused to digest this information. "Do they know?"

"Of course not! Mikhail kept shtum. Never logged it."

"Then he was a fool!"

"No, Oleg – he was prepared to take the chance – like me."

Medlyev's bushy eyebrows joined forces and formed an unbroken line across his forehead. "And?" he asked after giving Zhukhov's bravado some considerable thought. "What did *you* find?"

Fischer had to admit he'd found nothing. "I ran out of time," he said, hoping this passed as a reasonable excuse. "Mikhail dropped me way back from the outcrops. Said it was too dangerous to go closer."

Medlyev was nodding vigorously. "He was right. You need all the tolerance you can get to recapture a pod."

Fischer shrugged his acceptance of this and added a sigh for good measure. "I could've done it if I'd had more time, that's all."

Medlyev refused to be drawn further, his concentration fixed on the inhospitable but brilliant terrain gliding past outside.

Fischer wasn't going to give up that easily. "If you got the pod down nearer to that track, Oleg, I could make it to the canyon with a sled"

"No."

Fischer persisted. "Give me two circuits downside, Oleg. That's all I ask. Tell them we've spotted what looks like some strata shift. They'd buy that.

"No."

"Come on, Oleg. Just think – what if this crazy intern turned out to be right, eh? What if there's something worth finding out there…?"

Medlyev *was* thinking, Fischer could tell. Mention of his old rival Zhukhov had already set things in motion. Fischer could almost hear the cogs turning. Maybe, just maybe, he thought, it was worth pushing his friend a bit harder. He changed tack. "Look, Oleg," he said, playing the last card in his hand. "I'm not a rookie – I've done field trips before. Long term stuff with Elsenbach on Hebda. I know the routine."

Medlyev shook his head. "No, I can't do it. It's too dangerous. You'd have no backup down there if things went wrong."

Fischer shrugged. "Okay, I understand," he said, offering Medlyev a strained smile. "It's a big ask. Just thought you might be up for it."

Under the weight of Fischer's implication that he might

be somewhat lacking in the testosterone department, Medlyev crumbled.

★ ★ ★

Fischer settled the harness straps across his shoulders and felt the tug of the weight behind him as he leaned forward to take up the slack. Behind him, the hulk of the two-ton life-support sled responded as if it weighed no more than a toboggan on ice. "All set to go," he reported back.

Medlyev began the count-down. "Setting mission time to zero in thirty seconds and counting," he said, his accent much thicker over the headset. "Twenty-nine...twenty-eight...

"...zero."

"And marked," Fischer confirmed.

There was a pause. "Fischer, my friend..."

"What?"

"Take care. Remember what I said."

"I will. I won't let enthusiasm get the better of me."

"Make sure that it doesn't. We're not playing games here. You've got plus sixty-two hours. That's all. At plus thirty-one you have to be heading back to the pod. Do you copy that?"

"Yes, Oleg, I copy that."

"I'll pick up your progress reports from the pod's communication relay after the first circuit. Make them regular, Fischer. I don't want to be shitting bricks up here wondering what you're up to my friend."

"I won't let you down."

"Good hunting."

"Thanks."

The communication link began to break up and Fischer was almost glad when the static finally cut him off completely: Medlyev's nagging was getting on his nerves.

He was on his own now, the exhilaration of it pumping through his veins. It felt really good.

The long Gammodian dawn was starting to break with the first massive sliver of Helios V heaving itself up over the far horizon. On either side of the desert plain, the silicate strata embedded in the tops of the volcanic rocks of the mountain ranges blazed with light. For the next ninety-six Earth hours, Helios would inch its way across the sky, sending the temperatures soaring to a searing 436K at its zenith. In less than sixteen, Fischer knew it would reach around 350K. For now, the outside temperature on the helmet's heads-up display registered 274K above absolute zero, roughly 0°C. He should make the most of it. If he'd calculated right, he'd about four hours before he got within reach of the mysterious track he'd seen from the surveyor.

He set off, feeling the tug on the harness as the sled moved with deceptive ease across the sand behind him. Under his boots, the going was firm and the walking poles soon helped him set up a steady methodical plodding rhythm.

He remembered to pace himself and breathe slowly. The suit's cooling system would be working flat out once Helios cleared the horizon in six hours. No point in raising a sweat now.

He plodded on, passing the time day-dreaming about

the possibilities that lay ahead. All he had to do was find the track – and follow it into the canyon.

Helios climbed a little higher and Fischer pulled down the helmet visor as the first shafts of light slanted across the plain ahead of him.

After an hour, the timer on the heads-up display flashed amber. He stopped, unstrapped himself from the harness and took a thirty-minute break in the shadow of the sled.

Sucking on the feeder tube inside his suit and trying to ignore the blandness of the rehydration fluid, he surveyed the landscape. According to the pedometer on his left ankle he'd covered just over three miles. About what he'd expected, remembering his expeditions with Elsenbach, and not bad, considering he wasn't in training.

According to the monitor, the temperature was already 281K. Maybe he should deploy the solar array along the spine of the sled. It had to be done sometime. After twenty minutes, he felt rested. Better to do it now, he reasoned, when his own energy banks showed maximum capacity, than later, when tiredness might make him less co-ordinated and clumsy. Okay, deploying the array would slow him down, but not much. Five minutes here. Five minutes there. No problem over all.

At the end of the second pitch, he had to extend the sun canopy from above the air-lock at the front of the sled. Even with the visor down, the low light reflecting into his eyes from the sand in front of his feet was too bright for comfort. And combined with walking at a monotonously steady pace with nothing else to focus on except the occasional glimpse ahead, he realised the effect was becoming hypnotic.

With the track still potentially some way off, his mind had switched off. He found himself day-dreaming, remembering the heated arguments with Bateman in tutorials at the Faculty.

Bateman was the ultimate carbon-chauvinist. Dismissive of any suggestion there might be anything other than carbon-based life-forms in the universe, he'd steamroller his opinions over everyone else's, particularly Fischer's. Carbon's creative ability to shape-shift from stable solids to gases in its many and varied combinations with other atoms made it supreme as far as Bateman was concerned. "Why do you keep rabbiting on about silicon?" he would say, his voice raised in denunciation of Fischer's attempts to justify his assertions. "It has no metabolic function – and you know it."

Fischer remembered getting hot under the collar and refusing to back down. He'd countered with the well-known fact that polymers of alternating silicon and oxygen were far more stable than equivalent hydrocarbons in a sulphuric acid-rich environment.

Bateman had simply shrugged this off. "Look, Fischer," he'd said disparagingly. "You can't get around the basic facts that if you're talking cosmic abundance, carbon beats silicon ten to one. And I can tell you, I'd rather breathe out carbon dioxide than silicon dioxide any day of the week." Everyone had laughed: it was a cheap gibe because it was patently obvious the human body wasn't designed to exhale silica in any shape or form – quartz, agate or carborundum.

Fischer's attempts to get the argument back on course were always doomed, even when he challenged Bateman to explain how plants and primitive life forms on Earth managed to assimilate silica into their structures.

"I'm not talking diatomic algae or sponges, Fischer," Bateman would say. "I'm talking *intelligent* life." And that was that, as far as he was concerned.

The amber light marking the end of the third pitch pulled Fischer back into the present. He stopped and looked around him, aware he'd been on automatic for some time. Helios was still not fully above the horizon behind him, but the reflections off the sand were dazzling. He squinted against the glare, scanning the horizon ahead. The mouth of the canyon was more clearly defined now, its dark interior a black gash set against the brilliance of the entrance rocks.

A quick check of his bearings confirmed he should be somewhere near the track. Time to do some serious reconnoitring. He could catch up with his rest schedule later.

Releasing himself from the harness, he plotted a systematic search starting with the area immediately to the right of the sled, quartering the area in the methodical routine he'd learned from Elsenbach.

Just shy of three hundred paces out, he found the track. It was as clear as day. He must have been walking parallel to it for some time. Trying not to let is imagination run wild, he knelt down to take a closer look. It was no aberration. Something, about half a pace in width, had made its way across the sand, pushing it aside in its meandering progress towards the canyon. He leaned forward and placed a gloved hand on the ruffled surface, closing his eyes and trying to imagine what strange exotic creature had passed this way. His heart-rate doubled in seconds. Calm down, he told himself. Calm down.

For a while, it was difficult to think rationally, his head full of wild possibilities. Pulling himself back onto his feet, he planted the walking poles in the sand to give some measure of scale and took several images to relay back to the pod. The ruffled grooves running along the bottom of the track came out really well.

He lumbered back to the shade of the canopy and had a serious discussion with himself. He sucked on the feeder tube remembering Elsenbach's advice to remain focussed. On the surface, the temperature was hovering just shy of 305K and there was still at least another four hours before he needed to call a halt and pitch camp for the 'night'. The suit's cooling system would come under increasing strain, he recognised that. Taking himself beyond the safety limit and ignoring the rest schedule wouldn't help. He must resist the temptation to push on regardless just to get closer to the canyon. Arrive alive, Elsenbach would have said.

With that in mind, he gave himself a longer rest period and double-checked his portable supplies and functionality before setting off to follow the track. Deciding on caution, he unhitched the air-pack and swapped the half-used cartridge for a full one from the supply locker. He could keep the half-used cartridge as a spare. Satisfied everything else was fine, he clicked the harness back into position and set off.

Following the track, he discovered, was just as hypnotic as not having a track to follow. His eyes became fixated by its drunken progress as it weaved across the sand patterns, while his brain went off again into realms of fantasy trying to imagine what form of locomotion could possibly be responsible for producing it. Was something rolling over and over itself, like a tumbleweed? Was it sucking up the sand ahead of itself and dumping it behind, like a harvester? Was it being pushed? – or pulled? Neither, he decided. There were no other tracks.

No nearer reaching a satisfactory conclusion, he plodded on, the narrow mouth of the canyon now visibly closer, the inner recesses divided between intense light and impenetrable shade. He could just make out the jagged outline of the pink and white quartz jutting from the surrounding grey igneous rocks at its entrance.

A red warning light jolted him back into reality. Checking the timer, he was shocked to discover he'd automatically over-ridden the amber advisory signal twice; Helios was half-way into the heavens with the temperature outside close to 326K; and his air cooling system perilously close to slipping into the red zone. He was on the brink of over-heating and dehydration.

He brought himself up sharp, undid the harness, and sat down in the shade of the canopy sucking hard on the feeding tube. His heart was racing. He couldn't credit himself with being so unbelievably stupid. Now he'd stopped, his leg muscles had begun to tremble uncontrollably, and his vision, fixed for so long on the ground immediately in front of his feet, was blurred and unfocussed.

He closed his eyes, cursing his lack of self-discipline. The next thing he knew, he woke up to find himself slumped over, his head lolling uncomfortably against the side of his helmet.

He must pull himself together. All the function sensors registered exhaustion markers. No way must he be tempted into thinking he could carry on: his energy reserves were low; the pedometer told him his rate of progress had slowed dramatically over the last three pitches without him realising; and it would take what little energy he had left to get himself safely inside the sled.

He struggled to his feet, surprised by the tendency to lose his balance despite the low gravity, and irritated to find his gloved fingers more clumsy that usual when wrestling with the mechanism on the air-lock.

Once inside, while he waited for pressure normalisation, he rehearsed what he could say to relay back to Oleg. With his brain like mush, he finally gave up. He would compile his report in the 'morning'.

The green light on the control panel came on and he unfastened the helmet, finding his hair plastered to his scalp with sweat. When he pulled off the suit, his body was in much the same condition. He smelled like a dead cat but was past caring. Crawling through into the cramped living space, he set the buzzer alarm for plus eight, and collapsed gratefully onto the bunk. In a comfortable atmosphere of 20°C, with the gentle lisping of the air ventilation system whispering in his ears, he didn't even turn off the light before he fell asleep.

When the buzzer sounded, he awoke feeling remarkably refreshed.

Washed, shaved, and wearing a clean undersuit, he was ravenous. Over two nutritious breakfast pouches, he constructed his report to Medlyev. Apart from adding, "all systems functioning normally" and providing Medlyev with a read-out to prove it, he decided to stay shtum over his serious lapse in time-keeping.

Determined not to be so damned careless again, he double-checked all the connections and functions on his suit; refitted a fresh air pack, rehydration and waste-disposal units, and cleaned up the air in the living quarters before finally kitting up. It took more than an hour, but, with Elsenbach's sobering advice ringing in his ears, rushing these routines was not an option.

Outside, the Gammodian morning was well under way, the temperature heading towards the 340K mark.

Hoisting himself into the harness and retrieving the walking poles from where he'd casually discarded them, he leaned forward, took up the slack and set off. He was practically jerked off his feet. When he turned to find out why, it became crystal clear: while he'd slept, the front end of the sled's glider rails had sunk into the sand. Pulling harder was more likely to wedge them in further. The only option was to decouple the harness, refit it to the back of the sled and pull the damn thing out backwards with the help of gripper-boards rammed under the rails.

He cursed. If he'd had only half his wits about him before he'd crashed out the 'night' before, he'd have realised why he was so damned unsteady on his feet: the density of the sand had changed. It was much, much softer.

In a fine temper, he undid the harness, dumped the poles and floundered his way round the side of the sled to access the storage locker. Selecting the sand shovel, he pulled out half-a-dozen gripper-boards from their rack. Six should be enough, he reckoned, wishing whoever had been clever enough to design the damned things – with their multi-purpose, flexible, interlocking expandible plates that could be opened out, dismantled or reassembled into several different configurations – had also taken the trouble to check their connection points were easy to slot together wearing gloves.

Eventually, he got them aligned into two rows of three behind the gliders and started digging. It proved a frustrating exercise. With every shovelful, almost as much sand slid down the side of the hole as he'd dug out. The hole never seemed to get any deeper, just wider. After several abortive attempts, the only way he could make progress was by manoeuvring the gripper-boards under the shovel first. It took him more than three painstaking hours to get the boards rammed in far enough to stand any chance of pulling the sled free.

The 'morning' had gone. He slumped down under the canopy and consumed his liquid lunch watching his function levels settle back into the 'normal' zone. He knew he could ill-afford to lose so much time.

Still rattled, he hitched up the harness reins to the tow points at the back of the sled and heaved. The sled came out unexpectedly fast, like a rotten tooth, and he found himself executing a slow-motion free-fall, landing face down in the sand under the full glare of the sun. He lay there for a moment feeling ridiculous before struggling back up onto his feet.

With no apparent damage to either his suit or the sled, he took stock of the situation. He now had only ten hours left to follow the track, four of which should be spent back in the sled tucked up fast asleep.

★ ★ ★

He told himself he was being rational. He'd made all the necessary preparations to make the best use of the eight hours he'd got left, double-checked everything, and was convinced it was the right thing to do.

Ready to go at last, he remotely accessed the sled's communication system to the pod.

"Hi, Oleg," he said casually. "Listen, there's been a bit of glitch. Nothing too drastic, but I've had to change my plans." He logged his position and explained what had happened. "I've checked the terrain going forward for four-hundred paces along 180°, and there's no way I can chance taking the sled any further. So I've parked it up a couple of hundred paces back where the sand's more stable. It should be fine there.

"Now don't panic, Oleg. Listen – I'm going on. I've made up the emergency life-raft as a trek-sled. It's easy to pull and it's got everything I need to see me out and back in good time. As I said – don't panic. I know the routine. Elsenbach rules. My timer's on and functioning. I'll keep you informed when I take break stops.

"Copy and out."

He could only imagine what Medlyev's reaction would be when he got the message.

Strapping a couple of inverted gripper-boards onto his boots, he discovered he could almost ski across the sand if he kept up a reasonable pace, the walking poles steadying him as he went. Behind him, the trek-sled was little more than a minor inconvenience.

By the time he reported back at his first rest break, he'd covered almost five miles, although a couple of them had been clocked up wandering around trying to pick up the track again after a momentary lapse in concentration. When he logged in, he made light of this and of the fact he'd had to take a longer than scheduled stop to let the temperature inside his suit drop back. Outside, it had risen close to 360K.

By the end of the second pitch, it was 375K. Fischer unhitched the harness and took stock. Ahead, the jagged brilliance of the pink and quartz rock strata interspersed with dull grey pumice at the mouth of the canyon rose up in front of him. Taking shelter out of the heat inside the life-raft, he transmitted several images of the track and canyon entrance through the open flap to keep Oleg happy. "Should make it inside sometime during the next pitch," Fischer told him. "I'll keep you posted."

The meandering progress of the track continued to head towards the canyon.

As he got closer, Fischer noticed there were eddies of sand around the base of the entrance. They danced and shimmied, caught and lifted up on thin thermals created by the different temperature levels between the intense light and shade inside the canyon. They were strangely beautiful.

A few hundred paces further on and he was actually among them, the fine grains flitting against his visor then shying away again, teasing him to catch them. He found himself laughing. "Hey, Oleg," he said, switching on his communicator again. "Just watch this." And he took a whole string of images for Oleg's benefit, before realising the swirling sand was acting like a billowing net curtain, blocking his view of the way ahead, and when he looked down, he could barely make out his boots. The track he'd been following was nowhere to be seen.

He turned off the communicator, listening to his heart hammering. Think, he told himself sternly.

He discovered if he craned his neck back as far as the helmet would let him, he could just make out the canyon walls some way above his head. Logically, he told himself, once he got into the shadow, the thermals supporting the sandstorm wouldn't be there and maybe, with a bit of luck, he'd be able to pick up the line of the track again, however faint.

Deciding to carry on regardless however proved difficult. He kept tripping over the gripper-boards because he wasn't sure where he was putting his feet, and the whirling sand was beginning to make him feel decidedly giddy.

The amber light signalled it was time to stop and he didn't take much persuading. The only problem was it made no sense to open the life-raft and smother its contents with sand. So he remained standing, thinking how bizarre it was he was sucking on the feeder tube in the middle of a sandstorm. That is, he was thinking how bizarre it was until he realised the pouch had run out and needed replacing. Under the present circumstances, this was impractical. The life-raft carried only lightweight external connector pouches. Fine-grained sand would clog up an outside connector valve in the blink of an eye. Worse still, if it got inside the connector dock itself, it would almost certainly breach the air-tight seal and threaten the integrity of his suit. The same problem applied to the air pack. The display was already telling him one of the cartridges was low. Elsenbach Rule No.1: never travel with a low or empty air cartridge except in an emergency. Like it or not, Fischer knew he had to push on into the canyon, head for the shade and hopefully out of the sand.

He'd have done just that if other more distracting thoughts hadn't immediately popped into his head. What if the track he'd been following had stopped at the mouth of the canyon? What if it had veered off to the right? Or the left? What if, because let's face it, he'd been distracted by the dancing sand, he'd walked right past whatever he'd been following without even noticing? And – and this was the worst thought of all – what if he'd inadvertently *stood* on it? For a moment, he was paralysed, unable to move a muscle while the sand continued to flirt with him, ever more persistently.

He opened the communication link. "Hi, Oleg," he said, trying to keep his voice as calm as he could make it. "There's too much sand blowing around here at the entrance, so there's nothing much to report on right now. I'm heading further into the canyon to get out of it. Copy and out."

Cautiously, he bent down, groping around blindly trying to unfasten the gripper-boards from his boots. He hoisted them over his shoulder and tested the ground under this feet. It was still very soft.

He inched forward with extreme care. And then his boot came up against something solid.

His heart practically jumped out of his ribs. Looking down, he could make nothing out except swirling sand. Cautiously, because he could think of nothing better to do, he leaned forward to touch whatever it was. He was suddenly very conscious of his breath coming thick and fast – that an amber light was flashing – and he needed to calm down or he'd hyperventilate.

It took him a minute or two to get himself back together again.

Using the walking poles to steady himself, he leaned forward again as far as the suit would let him and reached out. His glove made contact with what felt like a rock – not a big rock – nowhere near as large as he'd expected. So it wasn't *his* rock. In fact it was just large enough for his fingers to wrap around the edges so he could pick it up without any problem. He shoved it close up to his visor, disappointed to discover it looked like a chunk of broken pumice: dull grey with lots of gas holes in it. Probably just debris dislodged from the canyon wall by a quake. He should have expected it.

There'd probably be more. Checking his immediate surroundings with the poles, he was irritated to find his assumption was correct: there seemed to be a whole batch of the damned things in the direction he wanted to go. There was absolutely no way he could haul the trek-sled over broken ground without it snagging against one damned obstacle after another. What the hell, he decided. If he looked up to the right, he was pretty sure he was about fifty – maybe seventy – paces away at most from an overhang. He could unhitch himself from the trek-sled, pick his way over there unencumbered and get himself under it without too much effort. With a bit of luck he'd be able to recce the area from there and see how far the sandstorm stretched into the canyon.

He activated the beacon on the raft, unhitched himself from the harness and inched his way to the right, nudging aside the rocks in his path with the side of his boots.

Eventually he reached the overhang and stepped into its shadow.

It was as if someone had flicked a switch. One minute he was out in the glare of the sun in a crazy swirl of sand; the next, he was out of it, standing in what looked like the mouth of a cave filled only with impenetrable blackness. But any hope that his problems were now behind him soon evaporated. Further along the canyon, where the dancing spirals of sand finally petered out, he could see the canyon floor was littered with piles of rock-fall. On the small tracts of sand between, there wasn't a single track to be seen.

Fischer just stared: he couldn't quite believe it. He didn't know whether he felt cheated or just plain angry.

Leaning back against the wall of the cave he swore loudly. That he should come so far and find so little! He could almost hear Medlyev mocking him. "What did you expect, Fischer my friend?"

"Please note," a calm but resolute female voice informed him, jerking him back to the present. "You have ignored your air pack amber warning for thirty minutes. Cartridge number one will cease functioning in less than ten minutes. You are advised to begin the substitution operation as soon as possible."

He acknowledged the warning, wondering why the hell he hadn't taken notice sooner. Elsenbach would've had his guts for garters.

Pushing himself upright, he dragged himself out towards the mouth of the cave.

At first, he wasn't sure he'd felt it: it was just a vague 'something'. A slight shiver in the ground beneath his feet. He stood stock still: waiting; wondering if he'd imagined it. And then it came again, only this time noticeably stronger.

A tremor.

He had to get himself outside into open ground. But he was already too late. Ahead of him, he could see chunks of rock from somewhere high up on the canyon walls falling with an elegant slowness past the entrance to the cave, crushing the pumice carpet on the canyon floor and embedding themselves in the sand.

Leaving the cave was no longer an option. There was nothing he could do but wait – and hope the tremor would pass.

As the ground continued to jar and judder beneath his feet, something very definitely nudged against his boot.

He peered down through the gloom, shoving back the visor to get a closer look, but he couldn't make out what it was. He activated the headlamp.

At his feet was a large lump of amorphous pumice, quivering. For one glorious moment, he thought it was alive until he realised it was responding to nothing more than the vibrations deep within the planet's shifting crust. Idly, he knocked it away with a deft flick of his boot. It rolled over a couple of times in a lazy sort of way before coming to an unsteady stop, caught in the pool of light from his headlamp. "Bloody thing," Fischer muttered to himself.

An aftershock, setting up a second rock-fall, diverted his attention for a moment. When he swung the beam back into the cave, he had to steady himself, not because the ground was still shuddering, but because he suspected he was seeing things. For a few minutes, he just watched, mesmerised. He needed to be certain. It wasn't long before he was. The ground had stopped shaking. Outside, the rock-fall had ceased.

The pumice was still quivering, and squeezing out of it through one of its narrow gas holes was a thin, dull metallic-grey, sponge-like object. It flopped onto the sandy floor of the cave, quivered again and expanded into its former self – a rock. Caught in the beam from the headlamp, a chain of bright white crystals buried deep within its fissures, blinked back at him. Then in no particular hurry, it continued its harvester-style progress across the sandy floor towards the back of the cave. Left behind in the sand was the familiar meandering track.

Almost hysterical, Fischer yelled triumphantly into the communicator, babbling incoherently and too delirious to care. "Hey Oleg, you old geocentric carbon chauvinist, what have you got to say for yourself now, eh? Just watch this!" And he sent off a stream of images to be relayed to the pod one after the other.

From where he was standing in the depths of the cave, it came as no surprise when the inevitable message, "Link not available," flashed up on the communicator.

"Damn it!" he said, stumbling back towards the entrance to retransmit.

"Link not available," came the reply.

Fischer looked up. Out in the brilliant daylight of the canyon, the landscape had been transformed. The dancing sand-storm had gone. In its place a thin grey mist of crushed pumice drifted unhurriedly to the ground like a discarded veil. Beyond, where he'd left the trek-sled, there was nothing but a jumbled mass of rock-fall strewn across a wide expanse of canyon floor.

It took a moment for Fischer to register precisely what this meant.